My name is Callum Ormond.
I am sixteen
and I am a hunted fugitive . . .

CONSPIRACY 365

BOOK TWELVE: DECEMBER

To James

First American Paperback Edition
First American Edition 2010
Kane Miller, A Division of EDC Publishing

Text copyright © Gabrielle Lord, 2010
Illustrations by Rebecca Young
Illustrations copyright © Scholastic Australia, 2010
Graphics by Nicole Leary
Cover copyright © Scholastic Australia, 2010
Cover design by Natalie Winter
Cover photography: boy's face by Wendell Levi Teodoro (www.zeduce.org)
© Scholastic Australia 2010; close-up of boy's face by Michael Bagnall © Scholastic
Australia 2010; castle © Gabrielle Lord. Internal photography: paper on pages 193,
192 and 168 © istockphoto.com/Tomasz Pietryszek; aged paper on page 024
© istockphoto.com/Mike Bentley

First published by Scholastic Australia Pty Limited in 2010
This edition published under licence from Scholastic Australia Pty Limited

All rights reserved.
For information contact:
Kane Miller, A Division of EDC Publishing
P.O. Box 470663
Tulsa, OK 74147-0663
www.kanemiller.com
www.edcpub.com

Library of Congress Control Number: 2009942503

Printed and bound in the United States of America
1 2 3 4 5 6 7 8 9 10
ISBN: 978-1-61067-114-9

CONSPIRACY 365

BOOK TWELVE: DECEMBER

GABRIELLE LORD

Kane Miller

A DIVISION OF EDC PUBLISHING

PREVIOUSLY . . .

1 NOVEMBER
The Special FX canister finally explodes, giving me enough cover to escape the ring of cops and the chopper. My hunters soon lock onto my position again, but my double—Ryan Spencer—comes to my rescue. We swap clothes, and he acts as a decoy, fooling the cops and luring them away from me.

2 NOVEMBER
The Caesar shift hasn't revealed anything hidden within the Ormond Riddle, and we wonder if it only applies to the missing two lines. Somehow, we must travel to Ireland, visit the Keeper of Rare Books, and investigate further.

Anxiety is high as Boges, Winter and I talk about the DMO. Just after we realize someone's hacked my blog, repeating "November 11" all over the page, we're interrupted by the arrival of cops—Winter's building is surrounded!

I make a terrifying leap from one rooftop to another and urge Winter and Boges to flee as well. On my run from Lesley Street, I stop by Ryan Spencer's apartment. It turns out his birthday is November 11—the mysterious date from my blog!

6 NOVEMBER
Nelson Sharkey thinks he can arrange a fake passport for my trip to Ireland. I hope that the remainder of my gold stash will cover the cost.

9 NOVEMBER
We need more money, so Winter decides she'll steal some from the cash-lined cigar boxes in Sligo's "scram bag," hidden in his closet.

11 NOVEMBER
The day my blog hacker warned me about has arrived. I'm too nervous to go anywhere, so I keep low in the treehouse that has become my latest refuge.

13 NOVEMBER
Boges and I wait outside Sligo's house as Winter attempts to steal his money while pretending to be over for a swim.

Winter arrives back at the beach rendezvous

point with good news—she snuck out ten thousand dollars for us!

14 NOVEMBER
Back at the treehouse, Winter tells me more about the day of her parents' fatal car crash. She wants to move on, but believes she can only do so after she's seen the wreck and confirmed whether the crash really was an "accident," or whether something more sinister was involved.

17 NOVEMBER
On my way to meet Eric Blair, I am captured by two burly thugs who take me to see Murray "Toe Cutter" Durham. Toe Cutter is deathly ill and wants to make a confession. He reveals that he was involved in the abduction of twin babies, years ago, and failed to dispose of them. After a scare with the police, the babies were separated. One was left behind—me—and later returned to the family, while the other was kept by Toe Cutter until adopted out illegally. This baby was Samuel—my twin—now known as Ryan Spencer.

Back at the treehouse, I call Mum to tell her Samuel is alive.

18 NOVEMBER
At the library I find another article about the

twin baby abduction. In it, Rafe was interviewed, showing a side of his relationship with Dad I had never seen. They used to be very close.

Finally I meet Eric Blair. I realize that he is the crazy guy from New Year's Eve who warned me I had 365 days to survive! Blair says he suffered an unknown viral infection and doesn't remember the incident!

20 NOVEMBER
While investigating Rathbone's list of nicknames, we discover that he will soon be heading to Dublin. He could beat us to the Ormond Singularity!

24 NOVEMBER
Eric Blair poses the question—what if the illness that killed my dad, and caused his own illness, was not a virus, but something deliberate?

29 NOVEMBER
The cops have taken Boges for questioning, Winter is scared, and Sligo is becoming increasingly suspicious. I receive a message from Winter, but before I can call her, I am tackled by police! Just as they are dragging me to the car, Sharkey appears and presents my fake passport, saving me with my new identity.

I now have a few missed messages from Winter,

but am spotted by Pepper Spray Cop and chased into a sports stadium with wild crowds of fans. Somehow I end up running onto the field with the players, and a massive close-up of my face appears on the big screen. The crowd is chanting my name as I'm pursued. I run down to the underground quarters and am forced to find a hiding place in a locker room. I jump inside an empty koala mascot costume—successfully hiding in plain sight when the cops search the place.

30 NOVEMBER

Rafe admits he believes I saved him at the chapel, and that he's been trying to protect me from the dangers of the Ormond Singularity.

While I'm waiting for Winter at the beach, Griff Kirby shows up, telling me that he saw her being tossed into a black Subaru. Sligo has her! We race to the scene of the kidnapping, then to Sligo's car lot. There we see Zombie Two locking up a shipping container—Winter might be trapped inside. Zombie Two and Bruno are alerted to our presence, and they attack. Before we know it, we're tied up and shoved into the container ourselves.

Griff makes a horrifying discovery—Winter's body, cold and lifeless. Her voicemail messages reveal that she'd found out that Sligo killed her parents by cutting the brake lines of their car. She confronted him, alone, because I didn't call her back. I wasn't there for her.

Now it's too late.

1 DECEMBER

31 days to go . . .

Car Lot

12:00 am

I couldn't move, couldn't speak, almost couldn't breathe. Winter's final words echoed through the black, suffocating space we were locked in, like a haunting message from the grave.

I held her slumped body next to mine. Her wild hair fell over my knees and onto the floor of the container. I tried to say her name, but all that came out was a croaking sound.

She'd saved my life so many times, and I had completely failed her. The one time she'd needed *me,* I had ignored her calls until it was too late. She was gone. The beautiful, raven-haired stranger who'd saved me from drowning in an oil tank was now dead.

If I'd been there for her—calmed her down and talked sense into her—she would never have confronted Sligo. She would have waited until it was safe. If I had answered just one of her calls, she wouldn't be lying cold and silent in my arms. She would still be alive.

A numbing sensation took over me as I rocked back and forth with her body in my arms.

"Cal!"

Griff was elbowing me in the ribs—his hands were still bound behind his back.

"Cal, let go of her!"

I shook him off. He was the last person I wanted to talk to right now, but he kept persisting.

"Let her go!" he shouted, shoving me with his shoulder.

I swung my arm out and pushed him away. "I don't want to let her go!" I shouted back at him, tears now stinging my eyes. "I won't let her go!"

"You have to, Cal."

"I don't have to do anything! Winter was my friend! She was—"

"She's breathing, Cal." Griff spoke over me as he steadied himself. "Breathing. That's all I'm trying to tell you. Listen."

I ignored him. I didn't want to hear his voice right now.

"Winter's *breathing*," he said urgently, kneeling closer to her. "Listen to me! Here, help me sit her up."

His words finally penetrated the blackness of my thoughts.

"She's breathing?" I repeated. As I spoke, I felt Winter stir.

I loosened my hold on her, and a second later her body convulsed into life. She started struggling, groaning, trying to pull away from me.

"Winter!" I gripped her shoulders, crazy with relief. "Winter? Are you OK?" I asked, trying hopelessly to keep my voice steady. "It's me! Cal!" I added, half-laughing, half-crying.

"Let me go!" she screeched, squirming with panic. "Get your hands off me!"

"It's me!" I said again. "You're OK, you're with me!"

"Huh?" she said, sounding dazed, as I helped her sit up. "What's happened? Where am I? Cal, is that you?"

"Yes, I'm here!" I squeezed both of her hands and tried to move her towards some moonlight that was creeping in through a rusty crack in the container.

"Where have you been?" she murmured.

"I'm *so* sorry I didn't call you back," I said, my guilt gushing out. "I'm sorry I wasn't there for you when you called. I just—" I stopped, not knowing how to explain myself. "I can't believe this; I thought you were dead a second ago!"

"Give her some air, Cal," suggested Griff. He

was awkwardly trying to rub Winter's arm to help warm her up. "She doesn't need to hear your apologies right now."

"Who's that?" asked Winter, squinting into the darkness of the container.

"You're in here with me and Griff Kirby," I explained.

"You and *Griff*?" she said slowly, bewildered and fearful. "What are you talking about? *Why*? Where are we?"

"We're all in the same boat," said Griff. "Or should I say *container*?"

"Container? Cal, what is he talking about?"

Winter tried to get up, but toppled right over.

"They must have drugged you," said Griff, helping her straighten up, "and you're still feeling the effects of it. I saw them dragging you into the black Subaru. You yelled out to me," he reminded her, as I worked on unwrapping the tape around his wrists. "You told me I had to go and get Cal."

"Yeah," she murmured. "From the beach."

"That's right," I said. "You told Griff he'd find me at the beach."

"And I did find him," added Griff, "but by the time we got back to the spot where you'd been shoved into the Subaru, all that was left behind were your things, scattered all over the road."

Winter began groping around in the darkness.

"We're in the car lot," I explained. "Griff and I came looking for you, but Zombie Two and Bruno caught us. Next thing we knew, they'd locked us in this container. You were already in here."

"We're in a *shipping* container?"

"Yep," said Griff. "On the back of a truck."

"Are they going to take us somewhere? How will we get out?"

They were questions we couldn't answer. Winter continued fumbling her way around the walls. She was nothing but a faint, wobbly silhouette in the darkness.

Next, she started banging, like she was testing the walls for a weak spot or a potential opening. Before long, Griff—whose hands were finally free—joined her.

"Help!" Griff shouted, as he thumped on the walls. "Let us out!"

The metal shuddered, sending reverberations around us.

"Help!" they both called out repeatedly, each cry more desperate than the last. "Help!"

It was getting louder and louder—Griff and Winter weren't letting up. Now they were both throwing themselves at the walls, like they were desperately trying to crack the container open. The noise was throbbing like a giant gong in my head.

I covered my ears—I couldn't take it any longer.

"Stop!" I screeched over the top of them. "Stop it! Banging on the walls isn't going to get us out of here! Would you both just calm down and think about this? There's nobody out there, and anybody that *could* be out there wants us to stay trapped in here! You're wasting your time!"

Winter and Griff slumped onto the metal floor. Silence returned to the container.

I stared into the blackness, hopelessly wondering how we were going to get out.

1:05 am

Finally, Winter broke the silence. "Cal, when I didn't hear back from you I just lost it. I wanted to talk to you so bad. I had the biggest news ever, and no one to share it with."

My stomach twisted with guilt.

"It was like everything inside me was boiling over," she continued, sounding increasingly agitated, "and I couldn't cool down. At first I was so relieved to have found the truth, but then fury took over! I always *knew* he killed my parents! I always knew it wasn't just an accident, and finally I'd found the proof. That lying murderer!" she screamed, kicking her boot into the wall.

"Hey," I said, softly, trying to calm her down again.

"My head was telling me the time wasn't right—it was telling me it would be stupid to confront him. But my heart couldn't wait. I knew he'd forged my dad's signature on the will, and I had the evidence to prove it. I'd also found our car in his car lot—more proof of foul play."

I shuddered at the thought of her facing up to Sligo. "And you found a drawing or something?" I asked, trying to recall what she'd said in her voicemail messages earlier.

"Remember when we first went searching together, I told you I was looking for a little something extra on the upholstery in the back?"

"Yeah," I said, "you mean the drawing of a bird or something?"

"A swallow. When I was about nine, I got into a ton of trouble after a long drive up the coast . . . I was bored, and I drew a small bird on the back seat of the car. As soon as I spotted our gold BMW in the yard, I crawled into the wreck and located the drawing scrawled on the seat fabric, just where I'd drawn it. It was faded, but it was there. That was our car, all right."

A sliver of moonlight fell through a crack and across Winter's face as she held her wrist up to look at her bird tattoo. No wonder it meant so much to her.

CONSPIRACY 365

Her hand abruptly fell back to her lap with a slapping sound. "So next I checked the brake lines," she said. "Those brake lines weren't worn down like the police reported—they'd been cut. Clean cuts—the sort made by sharp pliers. That car crash was no accident. It had nothing to do with the weather. It was—"

"—*murder*," I whispered.

"Somehow, after the crash, he must have swapped vehicles, replacing my parents' car with another one of the same make and model that *did* have worn brakes. So the police accident report didn't lie—it just described some other wreck."

"He must have broken into the secure police lot to do that," I said. "Or paid someone to do it for him."

"Sligo has his tentacles everywhere," she said. "He's proven he's capable of anything. Like I was saying, I charged over to his house and into his study in a fit of fury. He was sitting behind his desk, drinking from some fancy, gold-rimmed, glass tumbler. I started yelling at him, accusing him of forgery and sabotage. He denied it, of course. He brushed me off and told me to get out and stop being a drama queen."

"You should have gone straight to the police," I said.

"I realize that now. It's probably the dumbest thing I've ever done. He wasn't taking me seriously, so I showed him the proof I had—photos I'd taken on my phone—" Winter stopped talking abruptly. "*My phone!*" she screeched. "Do you have it?"

"Battery's dead," Griff answered quickly. "I just checked it a second ago . . . I can't believe I don't have *my* phone on me."

"*My* phone!" I shouted, practically throwing my bag off my back and fumbling over the floor for it.

As soon as I picked it up I tried to switch it on, but it too was dead. I'd forgotten to hang it up after hearing Winter's voicemail messages, so the battery had completely drained.

"Any good?" asked Winter hopefully.

"Nope."

Griff muttered.

Frustrated, I shoved everything back into my bag.

"So how did Sligo react to the photos?" I asked Winter.

"He looked at them, just to humor me at first, but once he realized what I had found, his pompous grin disappeared. He puffed up like a great big toad, purple with rage. He crushed the glass tumbler he was clutching with his *bare fist*.

I was so scared, I thought I was dead. He came at me with his eyes bulging and fists raised, and I snatched my phone away from him and backed off, thinking he was about to grab me and wring my neck!"

Winter paused and let out an exhausted breath.

"Then he changed," she continued. "As quickly as he'd blown up, he calmed down. He started laughing like he suddenly thought it was hilarious. He said I was as smart as he was—maybe even smarter—and that I should channel my talent and become a partner in his business. He promised to give me the money owing to me as long as I kept my mouth shut and as long as I sat beside him at his New Year's Eve ball like a perfect princess. He also said he was on the verge of making a whole lot more money."

"A whole lot more?" I asked, instantly panicking about him unraveling the DMO before us.

"He said he 'had to' reach the Ormond Singularity before the end of December," she explained, confirming my fears. "By that time I'd realized how much danger I was in, but I was all alone. No one knew where I was. I didn't have backup."

Her words hit me hard.

"I decided to play along, pretending that I was seriously considering his offer. I walked around, as if I was deep in thought, while he threw the shards of broken glass from his desk in the trash and poured himself another drink. He offered me a juice, and I nervously sipped on it as I paced the room."

"Did he say anything else about the Ormond Singularity?"

"The Ormond Singularity?" Griff was muttering to himself, clearly confused.

"Sligo kept raving on about how he needed to crack it so that he could display the Ormond Jewel around my neck at the ball and make his name as a great medievalist and antiquarian. I could be his 'equal partner.' He said the entire world would be at *our* feet. I was pretending to be impressed, but the whole time I was planning how to get out. I excused myself to go to the bathroom, then I bolted. I was on my way to the police station when I started to feel really weird—all weak and floppy. Every sound around me was fading, and my vision was going blurry. I sat down on some steps, thinking it must have been the heat. Then I remembered the fruit juice—Sligo had put something in it! Next thing I know, Bruno's dragging me off the street into the car. I kicked as hard as I could, but I couldn't stop him!"

"That's when I saw you," said Griff.

"Sligo made a final phone call to your cell," I said. "He didn't realize I'd picked it up from the road. He said enough for me to guess you'd been taken to the car lot. When we got here and I saw the container, I was pretty sure you'd be in it. Then Bruno and Zombie Two saw us—"

"And locked us in here with you," Griff finished for me, feeling around the container again. "We're all up to speed now, so how about we focus on getting out of here?"

Griff's suggestion was met with stifling silence. Clearly, none of us had any good ideas.

Outside the container and beyond the deserted car lot, the sounds of distant traffic hummed almost inaudibly.

Griff spoke again. "We're better off trying to escape now, while we at least know where we are. If this truck moves us, we could end up stacked like bricks in cement on a container ship in the middle of the ocean. We'd die there, for sure."

"I'm scared," whispered Winter.

1:29 am

I stood up and started pacing the length of the dark space of the container. If only there was something I could do. If only I could find some way to connect with the outside world. With Boges or—

"The distress beacon!" I shouted.

"The what?" said Griff.

"The micro distress beacon Boges gave you!" Winter shouted excitedly. She jumped to her feet and awkwardly hugged me.

"I have a distress beacon stowed in my shoe," I explained to Griff. "My mate Boges gave it to me, for use in an emergency!"

"And you've only just thought of it now?" he said, in frustrated disbelief.

"I'd almost forgotten all about it, but *who cares*?! It means we're getting out of here!"

I sat back down and wrenched my shoe off. "Once he realizes we're missing, he'll check the tracking program to see if we've activated the beacon. Then he can follow the signal to this container."

"But what about the police?" asked Winter. "They're watching him. What if they follow him here?"

"Boges will be vigilant. He knows how important our freedom is. But let's not worry about that right now; I have to get this beacon activated."

With shaking fingers, I pulled up the inner sole from my sneaker and started to rip away the tape. I located the beacon and pressed the tiny switch.

It didn't make a sound, but I had to believe it was working.

If Boges didn't activate his tracking system before this container was picked up and shipped out, I didn't like to think what might happen to us. Griff was right—we needed to get out before they moved us.

Now we had to play the waiting game.

9:01 am

"Who's that?" hissed Winter, grabbing my arm suddenly.

I froze and listened carefully. I could hear footsteps and the murmur of a voice approaching.

"Do you think it's Boges?" Griff whispered.

"Shh," I said, straining to hear whether the voice outside was familiar or not.

As it became louder, I recognized who it was.

It wasn't Boges.

It was Zombie Two.

"In the container," he said, loud enough for the three of us to hear. "We both come back tomorrow morning to remove."

We all shuddered as his voice moved away. Finally we heard a car driving off and hoped that meant Zombie Two had left again.

"Your friend had better get here before *they* do," warned Griff.

8:15 pm

The day blended into the night as the three of us huddled for hours and hours, anxiously waiting in the darkness of the container. All of us would jump at the slightest sound, hoping it was Boges coming to our rescue while fearing it was Bruno, Zombie Two or Sligo, back again to *remove* us.

But no one had come.

Eventually, Winter and Griff fell silent, and I could hear Winter's steady breathing beside me. The air inside the container was getting thicker and thicker.

I couldn't fall asleep—I was tormented with horrible thoughts. What if Boges didn't think to check up on his tracking program? What if the three of us were left here to die—from thirst and starvation—without anyone but the people who put us here ever knowing? What did Sligo plan on doing with us tomorrow morning? I didn't want to stick around and find out.

The way I'd felt when I'd held Winter in my arms earlier, thinking she was dead, wouldn't leave my mind either. I needed the chance to make a lot up to her. She'd been through so much, and she'd been so brave. And now, just when she had the evidence she needed to get Sligo right out of her life forever, and claim what was rightfully hers, she was trapped.

Guilty. I felt so guilty.

Because of me, Boges had been picked up and questioned by the police. For all I knew, they could have arrested him by now. Because of me, his future was uncertain. On top of that, I'd only just realized that I'd forgotten his birthday.

2 DECEMBER

30 days to go . . .

8:26 am

"Hey," said Griff, shaking me. I must have finally dozed off to sleep. "There's someone outside! They're here! That big guy's come back like he said he would!"

I sat up, alert. He was right—I could hear footsteps.

"Can't you hear it? Winter, wake up!" Griff shouted. "They're here!"

"Shh!" I hissed. "If it *is* Sligo we don't want him knowing we're all still alive!"

That quieted him. He crouched down silently.

"Someone's here?" Winter asked in a low voice, only just waking up.

"Sounds like it," I whispered. "Zombie Two said they'd be back in the morning, so if it's them, then the minute the doors are opened we all need to charge out as fast and as hard as we can. It's our only hope. If we all charge together, one of us might make it past them and be able to get help. OK?"

"OK," agreed Winter and Griff.

"Ready?"

"Ready!"

We braced ourselves, ready to spring as we heard the clanging and creaking of the heavy container doors opening.

As fresh air gushed towards us and daylight shone in, I squinted and flew at the two silhouettes before us.

I took down the first guy, knocking him hard to the ground. Bodies thudded and struggled beside me too.

"Hey! Easy, dude, it's me!" Boges shoved me off him.

"Boges!" I said. "Man, I am so sorry!"

"Get off me!" I heard a familiar voice grunt beside me. It was Nelson Sharkey. Griff and Winter had both tackled him and pinned him to the ground.

"We didn't know whether the distress beacon would work!" exclaimed Winter, helping Sharkey to his feet before running over to hug Boges. "We're so glad to see you!"

"You should never have doubted my craftsman-ship," scoffed Boges, dusting off his notebook and straightening his shirt.

My eyes were slowly adjusting to the light as I scoped the car lot. Sharkey's car was parked just outside the entry gates. I couldn't see any sign of Sligo or his goons, but I knew they could turn up at any moment.

"Let's get out of here," I said, hauling up my backpack.

8:37 am

We crawled, one after another, through the opening in the fence that Sharkey had made with bolt cutters, then piled into his car and took off, skidding and screeching.

"As soon as I realized you were both MIA," said Boges, "I immediately opened the program for the distress beacon. The second I saw your signal I called Nelson. He picked me up and helped me trace you. It didn't take us too long to track you down to Sligo's car lot."

Sharkey pulled the car over to drop Griff off, not too far from his aunt's hotel near the docks. We'd driven past a huge Christmas tree decorated with tinsel and golden boxes tied up with gleaming ribbons that had been set up in the park nearby. I could hardly believe it was almost Christmas. That meant the end of the year was way too close for comfort.

"I'll call you," said Griff, as he climbed out of the car. "But not too soon, OK?"

I understood—Griff and I were both guilty of

bringing trouble to each other, but without him I never would have found Winter.

"Thanks!" I shouted, as he ran away into a crowd of shoppers.

"OK," said Sharkey, from the driver's seat. "Where to next?"

Winter looked at me apprehensively from the front passenger seat. She opened her mouth to say something and then stopped.

"Your place?" Sharkey asked her. "I think I remember where that is."

Winter shook her head, and it hit me. Now she was like me. She couldn't go back to her apartment. She didn't have a home anymore. Neither of us did.

"Let's go to Lovett's," Boges suggested, like he was reading my mind.

I nodded.

He gave Sharkey directions while I wondered if I could ever pay my friends back.

"Boges," I said quietly. "Sorry I forgot your birthday. Next year will be different, I promise."

Treehouse

10:20 am

Sharkey dropped the three of us off on the road that led to Luke Lovett's place. Before he drove away, I asked him, "Nelson, when you were working on a tough case in the police force, and you ran up against a brick wall, what did you do?"

Nelson leaned his elbow on the window ledge. "I began again, Cal. Went back to the start. The PLS."

"The PLS?" I asked, aware of Boges and Winter listening attentively beside me.

"The Point Last Seen. If it's a missing person, you go back over the investigation. You go back to the place where they disappeared. You re-interview people, you ask for other witnesses to come forward. You hope to find fresh clues that maybe you'd overlooked before. Walk-throughs are really helpful because memory is state dependent."

"Meaning?" Winter asked.

"You know when you're in the house, and you're walking to a room to get something, and by the time you get there you forget what you were looking for?" Sharkey continued.

"Yep," we all answered.

"Then you retrace your steps to where you were standing or sitting when you first got the idea, and then suddenly it pops back into your head again—it's like doing that," said Sharkey. "Now are you guys set? I have to keep moving. I'll look into flights for us all and get back to you, OK?"

"Cool. Thanks again," I said, as he drove off, leaving just the three of us, disheveled and relieved.

"Winter, you'd better hang with me until you've organized another place Sligo doesn't know about," I said, as we all crept towards the back of Luke's place.

I saw the strain and exhaustion in her face. The happiness that had shone in her eyes as we were freed from the container was long gone. I'd been living rough for almost a year now, but she'd been living on a razor's edge, keeping her secrets and suspicions from Sligo, for the last six years. All while practically living in the dragon's den.

"It's OK, Winter," I began, reaching for her shoulder.

"It's not OK," she said, shaking my hand off. "All my stuff is back at the apartment and I can't go back and get it. I'm used to being alone, but now I have nothing. Nothing. My bag was smashed on the road when I was hijacked, I don't have a phone, and we have to get to Ireland, and it'll be freezing there. I have no clothes, and I'm filthy!"

"I have your phone," I said, digging it out of my backpack. "It just needs charging."

She took it, and we continued walking.

"Cal and I will break into your apartment," said Boges, bravely. "We can try and pick up your stuff for you."

We pushed through the bushes that formed the back boundary of the Lovetts' property and hurried over to the massive tree at the back, huddling together under its wide canopy. I reached up and yanked the rope down from where it had been thrown up out of the way over a low-lying bough.

Winter sighed as she climbed the rope. "Here I go again. Gorilla girl and the monkey boys. So where's the bathroom?" she asked, once at the top.

I pointed to a faucet near the back fence.

"You're joking."

I shrugged.

Boges hauled himself up into the treehouse. "Peaceful hideaway, leafy grounds. Open plan for easy living. Carpeted throughout. Bright and airy. Loads of character."

"Exactly," I said. "Not so bad."

"*Character* is a word real estate agents use when a place needs to meet a wrecking ball more than a new tenant." She sat down cross-legged on the bench and tied her hair back with a rubber band from her wrist. "I have to go back to my apartment. I have to get my passport at least, otherwise going with you guys to Ireland and cracking the Ormond

Singularity will be nothing but a dream for me."

"Like Boges said, we'll watch your apartment and if it's safe," I said, "we'll retrieve your things for you."

The color suddenly drained from Winter's face. "The money! I don't have the money!"

"Where is it?" Boges asked, alarmed.

"Back at the apartment! What if Sligo's already found where I've hidden it?"

"Where'd you hide it?" I asked, hoping it wasn't just in a drawer or something.

"Inside the sofa. It's not the best hiding spot, but maybe he won't look in there unless he's realized the cash from his scram bag is missing . . ."

"We'll find out soon enough," said Boges. "We're gonna have to go there tonight."

12 Lesley Street

9:45 pm

Boges and I squatted in the darkness across the road from Winter's building. We checked out every parked car to make sure they were empty. Once we'd confirmed there was no one watching the building from the outside, and that there was no sign of Sligo, Bruno or Zombie Two, we snuck over to the fire escape stairs and silently made our way up.

The key to Winter's door wasn't working.

"Let me have a try," said Boges. But he couldn't turn it either.

"Sligo's changed the locks already," I hissed, glancing around us nervously. "We'll have to break in."

Above us, the stars, dull because of the pollution from the city, twinkled faint and distant. An airplane coming in to land over the sea soared overhead.

"Watch out," I said to Boges, as I picked up one of the potted plants Winter had growing at the front of her tiny apartment. Taking advantage of the roaring of the airplane, I smashed the potted plant through the window.

The shattering glass still sounded deafening, and we froze, nervous someone had heard it and would come to investigate the noise on the roof.

Nothing happened. No one came.

I carefully knocked out the remaining glass fragments and climbed inside, then unlocked the door for Boges.

Using flashlights, we found our way to the sofa, digging our arms in under the cushions, searching for the hole Winter had told us was there. I pushed my hands around, grazing my fingers on rough, iron springs.

"Anything?" Boges asked anxiously.

I shook my head.

My grasping fingertips finally felt something—wads of folded bills, held by rubber bands.

"Got it!" I said, pulling them out, one by one.

"Hurry, dude," said Boges, who was now up and standing guard at the smashed window, looking out into the night. "I don't want us to be here one second longer than we need to be."

I didn't need any urging. I shoved the wads of money into my backpack on top of my fake passport and then started looking for the things Winter had asked us to get. I grabbed her phone charger and scooped up some clothes from her drawer, while Boges grabbed her sleeping bag and things from her bathroom.

Boges pointed his flashlight to a spot on the ground. Lit up were the two photos of Winter's parents, both lying crookedly in their frames under shattered glass.

"Sligo must have trampled them in a rage," said Boges.

I saw a copy of *The Little Prince* lying nearby and impulsively picked it up and shoved it in my backpack.

"I can't find her notes," whispered Boges, shining the light over the desk where Winter had said she had left them. "Where could they be?"

Our eyes met over the empty table.

"Sligo," we said, our voices overlapping.

Treehouse

10:51 pm

"So Sligo has all our information on the Ormond Singularity?" Winter cried.

I nodded. It was just the two of us in the treehouse. Boges had gone home after the Lesley Street raid, leaving me to make the trek to the treehouse alone.

"But Cal," she argued, "Sligo could join Rathbone in Ireland, and the two of them could go straight for it! Forget about the Jewel and the Riddle! They can do everything *we* planned on doing—using the photos and other clues to find the location!"

"We can't give up now. Nobody has the last two lines of the Riddle."

"*Yet*," said Winter. "And we don't have them either." She unrolled her sleeping bag and laid it out. It took up almost a third of the floor space.

A wave of anxiety unsettled my guts. "At least we have the money, right?"

"We do have that. Thanks for getting my other stuff too," she said, reaching into the box in the corner for a couple of granola bars Boges had left behind. "Did you see the photos of my mum and dad?"

I pictured them, trampled on the floor. "I'm sorry, I forgot to grab them," I lied. "I'm going back to the PLS," I said, changing the subject and tearing the wrapper off the bar she'd tossed me.

"The point last seen of your original backpack? The bag containing the Jewel and the Riddle?"

"Right," I said.

"Which means a second visit to Rathbone's? The undertakers'?"

"Right again. I've been thinking about what Sharkey said about memory being state dependent. If I reenact my last visit there, I just might remember what that familiar smell was. Plus we need to search the place. Crim's often hide stuff with their families. Maybe Sheldrake Rathbone has stored something there that will give us a clue as to where my bag went, or something that might help us uncover the identities of Deep Water, Double Trouble and the Little Prince," I added, as she leafed through the white book I'd brought back for her. "Until Sharkey books our flights, there's not much else we can do."

11:11 pm

Winter curled up and went to sleep, while I worried about Sligo and Rathbone getting together in Ireland and beating us to the truth. We *couldn't* let that happen. Things Rafe had revealed to me in our phone conversation last month repeated in my head too.

"I've got it!" yelled Winter, abruptly kicking her sleeping bag off and sitting up. "Cal," she whispered now, remembering to keep her voice down. "How could we have been so *stupid*?"

I jumped up and almost banged my head on the low ceiling. "What are you talking about?"

"I know who the Little Prince is! I can't believe it's taken us so long to figure it out!"

"Who is it? Tell me!"

"Just think about it," she said, reaching for the nearby book. "It has a boy all alone, a crashed airplane, drawings, a rose, adults who can't be trusted . . . The boy is a prince from a faraway place. A prince is someone who inherits a title, riches, someone who is an heir. Who does that remind you of?"

"Me," I whispered. "I'm the Little Prince on Rathbone's list." I looked at her, dumbfounded. "Rathbone must think it's possible I have the Riddle and the Jewel."

"And *we* know you don't," Winter continued. "So that only leaves Deep Water and Double Trouble."

3 DECEMBER

29 days to go . . .

Temperance Lane

9:37 pm

We were across the road from Rathbone, Greaves and Diggory—the funeral parlor. Inside the store a soft light was glowing, suggesting someone was still in there. The rest of the street was dark and empty, apart from a few parked cars. Nothing stirred, not even a cat.

"By the way," said Boges quietly, "I visited Gabbi today, and she convinced me to give her your phone number. She's promised not to give it to anyone else and promised me she wouldn't use it unless it's an emergency. I hope that's OK."

"Sure," I said, hoping it wouldn't get either of us into any trouble.

We shrank down as the lights in the storefront went out, then scrambled around the back of the premises through the gate and huddled behind a dumpster, carefully waiting to see who was leaving.

Eventually the back door opened, and a thin, weedy guy stepped outside, turned back and locked up.

I'd never seen him before. He walked away from us, in the direction of a car. Within minutes, he'd driven off.

"Come on," said Winter, creeping out of the shadows and running over to the door. She waved her hands, gesturing to us to follow her. "Hmm, this lock is not going to be easy."

"Maybe this isn't such a good idea," said Boges, looking over his shoulder to the street. "I don't like the thought of all those stiffs lying in there. Plus I don't want to *become* one of them, if we're caught!"

Winter pulled a metal nail file out from under her sleeve and started poking it around the lock.

"Hurry, please," urged Boges. "Let's get this over and done with."

"Must be a *dead*lock," joked Winter, as she struggled to get the door open.

Boges's face was serious.

"Not funny," he said.

"Whatever it is, I can't do it," she said finally. "This is a serious lock. My nail file can't compete with it."

The sound of a car made us bolt from the door and across to the cover of the dumpster again. It was the weedy guy. He must have forgotten something. We watched him get out of his car, approach the back door, unlock it and disappear inside once more.

"He's left the door open a crack," I whispered. "Now's our chance. He probably won't be in there for long. Come on, Boges. The three of us could take on that little guy if we had to."

Winter tugged Boges's arm as we snuck over to the door. I peered in and could see a light on in the office area.

"Quick, follow me," I hissed to my friends, before stealthily leading them inside the dark, short hallway and towards the showroom. I remembered the layout from my last visit, shivering from the memory.

We crept into the main showroom, walking directly past the office where the weedy guy was. I could hear him shuffling papers in there. The light from the office discreetly touched on the rows of coffins and caskets on display.

The three of us ducked down in the furthest corner, behind a long counter draped with lacy fabric, presenting an open coffin on its surface.

"What's that funny smell?" Winter asked.

"Probably embalming fluid," shuddered Boges.

"Gross," Winter whispered beside me.

"Shh," I hissed at them, as the light in the office went out, and footsteps clicked across the floor.

We waited until the door was locked from the outside, and the car drove away, before we emerged from our hiding place.

"I'm going to search the office," I said.

"I'll help," said Boges. "I'll start on the cupboards."

"I'll do the desk," Winter offered.

10:03 pm

"Nothing," said Boges, after he'd finished with the cupboards.

"Nothing here, either," said Winter, straightening up from the desk. "Just catalogs of coffins, caskets and artificial wreaths. What's that?" she asked, alerted by a sound from the back of the building. "Don't tell me that scrawny guy's forgotten something else!"

"It's nothing, just someone getting into their car," I said. "Boges, what if this place has a back-to-base alarm?"

"Then we're in big trouble," he said. "Let's get a move on. Let's see if that painted coffin is still here—that was about the last thing you saw before you blacked out, right?"

"That's where my bag was thrown."

"Wait—what if someone's," Boges paused to clear his throat, "living in there?"

"*Living*'s not the right verb," Winter corrected

him. "Besides, these are just display coffins," she said. "Just samples. People look at them and then order the one they like. They're empty." She began giggling and flapping her arms like a chicken, until Boges gave her a shove.

We moved back into the display area, and I waved the beam of light from my flashlight around the showroom until it landed on the familiar white coffin with its Sistine Chapel skies and angels inside it.

"That's the one," I said. "I walked up to what I thought was a counter, here, like this," I explained, reenacting the steps I had taken on that July night. "The envelope I had come for was sitting on top of it, so I picked it up and then bam!"

I jumped back, illustrating the force of the impact that had knocked me off my feet.

"The counter was actually a coffin. Somebody flew out of it, and before I could do anything I was overpowered and jabbed in the neck with some sort of drug. I started trying to get up, but I was too groggy. All I saw was my backpack being chucked into that coffin over there."

I stood still, closed my eyes and took a deep breath. Then something amazing happened.

I spun around to my friends. "The smell! I almost had it! Sharkey was right! By retracing my steps and standing here just like I did last time, and *feeling* the way I did last time, it almost came back to me!" I said. "It's like a sneeze that won't burst out! It's so frustrating! It's on the tip of my—"

"Nose?" Winter suggested.

Boges looked like he wanted to shake the answer out of me.

"I almost had it, really."

I walked away from the coffin and then turned, retracing my footsteps once more. Maybe one more approach would trigger the deep, unconscious memory that lurked somewhere in the back of my mind.

It was no use. That initial powerful surge towards remembering didn't happen again. Instead, it faded on me.

A howling shriek from Boges instantly snapped my attention his way. Winter and I shone our flashlights on him—he was flat up against the wall, as white as a ghost.

"I thought you said there weren't any bodies in here!"

"There shouldn't be," Winter said, peering into the open coffin Boges was backing away from. I looked over her shoulder. *A bloodied corpse?*

The sound of a vehicle being driven up and parked out in the back made us freeze again. We ran to the rear door and flattened ourselves on either side of it.

I peered out the window and spotted a van.

Boges's eyes were even wider with fear.

"I think someone's about to come inside," I hissed, hearing the van door open and close just yards away. I pressed against the wall, shaking with tension. "Stay quiet, wait till they've stepped all the way through the door, then the three of us bolt out and turn left down Temperance Lane. OK?"

My friends nervously nodded.

The sound of something being unloaded outside was quickly followed by the approach of footsteps, the jangle of keys and the twisting of the rear-door handle. We watched the handle turn, then the door opened slowly.

In the soft glow of the streetlight I spotted the gleam of the front end of a chrome-plated collapsible dolly. It was wheeled awkwardly through the doorway, followed by the stooped figure pushing it.

As soon as the guy and the dolly were in, I gave the signal to my friends.

He let out a terrified scream as the three of us sprang out of the darkness, shoved past him and ran out the door.

We pelted through the alley and down the street.

"Poor guy," said Winter, as we raced away,

"must have thought some of the deceased had escaped! I hope he doesn't die of heart failure!"

10:34 pm

"What was that bloody body doing in there?" asked Boges, as we all caught our breath in a deserted churchyard. "Were they bullet wounds?"

Before I could answer, I felt my phone vibrating in my pocket.

My friends nodded to me, urging me to answer it.

"Yes?" I said firmly.

"Cal!"

"Gabbi?" I said, instantly alarmed. "What is it? What's wrong?"

"You've got to come!"

"Calm down and tell me what's going on."

"The voices woke me up!"

"Whose voices?"

"Mum and Uncle Rafe—they were yelling at each other. Mum was going nuts and screaming about something, and Rafe was trying to calm her down. Cal, I think she's really lost it. Uncle Rafe must have come home late—he wasn't home when I went to bed. I don't know how it all started, but when I got up I saw Mum all red in the face, angry and upset. She was chucking things around!"

"It's OK, Gab, everyone has fights. Really big

ones sometimes. They'll calm down and forget all about it."

"I don't think so. This is big, Cal. Mum ran right out of the house. I thought she'd left me behind!"

"Mum would never do that," I said, unconvincingly.

"Rafe raced out after her, begging her to relax and come back. He wanted her to take her medication. She just told him to get away from her, then she ran back into the house and grabbed me from where I was on the stairs. I was really scared. She dragged me out the back, then we climbed into the car and drove off. Rafe was yelling out the front door that she shouldn't be driving in that state. It was horrible!"

"Where are you now?" I asked.

"Marjorie's place. Marjorie helped calm her down. They're out in back talking now. Mum's still crying, I think. I tried to hear what they're saying . . . but—"

"Where's Rafe?"

"I don't know, we just left him standing in the dark, outside the house. Cal, I don't know what to do—Mum's not the same as she used to be. She's never lost it before like she did tonight. Can you please come and see me?" my sister cried.

I didn't know what to do.

"Please, Cal!" she begged, in between sobbing and sniffling.

"I'll come around as soon as I can," I decided impulsively. I hated hearing her sound so upset. "You'll have to sneak out front to meet me. Nobody can know about this. You'll have to be very careful, OK?"

"OK."

I hung up the phone and turned to the others.

"We're coming with you," they said together.

"I'll be quicker alone," I said, "and more discreet. I'll meet up with you both at the cenotaph in two, maybe three, hours?"

"Cool," said Boges. "Hey, look, a taxi's coming. It'd be a lot quicker than walking from here to Richmond . . ."

"I'm grabbing it," I said, making a rash decision and rushing out to the road.

"Are you sure?" asked Winter. "It'll be faster, but it might not be safe."

I nodded, flagging down the taxi. I needed to get to Gabbi as fast as possible. "Let's hope the taxi's a good omen."

Flood Street, Richmond

10:43 pm

I hung my head low and paid the driver. Luckily

he'd been completely focused on a phone call to another driver that he was taking on speaker. I climbed out, and he drove away, leaving me at the end of my old street.

I tried not to look at our house as I passed it, now inhabited by strangers. It sat there surrounded by bushes and trees that were so much taller than I remembered.

Gabbi was waiting for me behind Mum's car, parked outside Marjorie's house. She threw herself at me and hugged me so tight it felt like I was being smothered by a small bear.

"Hey, hey, steady, Gab," I gasped, as she squeezed me. "It's OK. I'm here now." I eased her off me and ducked down with her behind the car again.

"But I don't want to stay here," she said, her eyes bloodshot from crying. "I want to go back to Mum and Uncle Rafe's place. I feel weird here."

I took her hands in mine. "Gab, you might have to stay here at Marjorie's until Mum sorts out whatever problem she's having. You can go back home later."

Gabbi's eyes shone with tears as she swung around and pointed over to our old house. "*That*'s my home! That's where I want to go! I want it to be back to when we were all together again, living there in our real house, just like it used to be before Dad died. Before all those bad things happened to you . . . and before Mum changed . . . and went crazy."

I put my arms around her. "We'd all love that, Gab," I said helplessly, as she snuggled into me.

Then she leaned back to look me in the face. "Please come home soon, Cal. I hate not having you around. It's so quiet. I miss my brother."

"I promise it won't be like this for much longer. But for now, both of us have to stay strong. I know it's not easy, living with Mum the way she is right now, but having Rafe helps, doesn't it?"

"It does," she nodded. "He's all right. I never liked him much before, but he's different now. *Better* different. He's been getting along so well with Mum—he still wants to marry her, you know—but you should have heard her yelling at him tonight."

"What was it about? What set her off?"

"I don't know, she wouldn't tell me anything. Rafe called Marjorie a few minutes ago and said he was going to come by as soon as he'd picked up Mum's prescription. He said he was on his way to a twenty-four-hour pharmacy in the city."

That trip would take him at least an hour, I figured. It gave me an idea.

"Gab, I have to go now. Look, you and Mum will be OK." I thought about the 365-day countdown and looming deadline. No matter what happened to me, this mess was going to be over soon, one way or another. "Go back inside. We'll see each other again soon."

"OK," she said, her voice muffled by tears once more. "But where are you going to go now?"

"I have something I need to check out," I said, not wanting to give too much away, "and then I'm going to meet Winter and Boges at Memorial Park."

Gabbi hugged me and touched the Celtic ring on my finger before sneaking back into the house. She glanced over at me one last time as she quietly closed the door.

I started sprinting towards Dolphin Point. There was something I really wanted to check out there, and time was going to be tight.

Rafe's House
Surfside Street, Dolphin Point

11:40 pm

There was no sign of Rafe's car outside his house, but there was a light on inside. I was hoping that in the craziness of Mum and Gab's exit, Rafe had simply forgotten to turn off the lights and more importantly, forgotten to set the security system.

I raced around the back to the patio, and my

eyes darted to the glass doors. They *were* open!

I held my breath as I eased the doors wider and stepped through.

Silence. The alarm was *not* on.

The living room was a mess. Mum's favorite purple mug lay on the floor in pieces, the remainder of her herbal tea forming a small, wet, brown puddle in the middle of them. Books and papers were scattered all over the place, as if someone had been impatiently looking for something, sending everything flying without care. Or was this just proof of Mum's irrational outburst, when she'd gone crazy like Gabbi had said, throwing things around?

Mum sure had changed over the last year. She'd never been the sort of person to lose her temper and throw things. She used to have everything under control. She used to be calm. She used to be reasonable.

Mum *used to* be a lot of things.

Rafe's old photo albums were stored on a low bookcase next to his vinyl records. I'd noticed them when searching through his house before, but I'd never actually stopped to look at any of the pictures inside.

In the last few weeks, so many things had happened that made me curious about Rafe. It was almost like he'd lived two completely different lives. The "Twin Tragedy" article I'd read for instance, where he'd spoken sadly of my missing twin, and lovingly of his own twin, my dad, had made me look at him differently. Even Eric Blair had said that in college Rafe was always by my dad's side. Everything pointed to him living a completely different life before the abduction—before Samuel was taken and before I was returned.

But was it true?

Rafe had admitted knowing I had come to his "rescue" at the Chapel-by-the-Sea, and he also knew so much more about the DMO than I ever realized.

I cleared space on the floor beside the shelf, kicking some loose papers out of the way. I knelt down and pulled out a couple of the fattest albums and began turning their pages, all the while listening carefully for the sound of a returning car.

The first album was filled with photos from Uncle Rafe's wedding. There were mostly pictures of him with Aunt Klara, posing together. Rafe was smiling in the pictures, but I could almost see something like sadness in his eyes.

I didn't know Aunt Klara that well before she died. From what I remembered, she was pretty quiet and kept to herself, even though she seemed nice enough. I never really thought about how lonely Rafe must have been after he lost her.

I slotted the wedding album back into place on the shelf.

The next album I opened was older and dustier. Right away I recognized Rafe and Dad together when they were young, probably about my age. I frowned, looking at them more closely.

In almost every photo, Dad had his arm over Rafe's shoulder, or the other way around. They both wore wide grins. They looked identical. They looked happy.

I pulled the album closer and flicked through it, eager to see more. Photo after photo showed the pair together: making silly faces and poses; blowing out candles on shared birthday cakes; dressed up in matching powder-blue suits at friends' parties; proudly holding their surfboards. There must have been hundreds of photos of the pair.

Rafe's words returned to me: "A special bond," he'd said, about being a twin. I sat back on my heels.

I frowned over pages of baby photos I recognized were of me, hauling myself up by a chair leg and standing up. My dad and Rafe stood side by side in the background. I wondered for a second about the discolored squares in the album, where pictures had been removed . . . before realizing that Rafe must have taken out all the shots of Samuel.

There wasn't much more to see after that. There were a few random shots of plants and buildings, but it seemed like Rafe had lost interest in tracking his life.

As I placed the last of the albums back on the shelf, an unopened envelope fell out from one of the film negative pockets.

Curious, I read who it was addressed to.

Tom Ormond.

On the back was Rafe's name and old address. Why had it been returned? Why had Dad never read it?

Carefully, I pried it open.

Tom,

You must stop blaming yourself for
what happened to the boys. It wasn't
your fault. It wasn't anyone's fault.
Collum will stop pining for his little
brother soon. I know it's tough to
hear it, but he's lucky he's young enough
to forget he ever had a twin.

Losing little Sam's been hard on me, too.
I know he's not my son, but you know how
much I love those boys. I love them
like they're my own.

I understand if seeing me at the moment
is too much for you — if it brings up too
many difficult thoughts of your lost son
and the fact that Callum may never have
what you and I have. Soon, when time
has helped heal the wounds a little, I hope

you'll be able to let me back into your life again. Like old times. Shutting me out is not going to make things easier for you, Tom.

I know the timing is terrible, but Klara and I have decided to go ahead with our wedding. I'd still love for you to stand by me and be my best man, but if you can't I will accept your decision.

Hoping you'll say yes.

Your brother,

Rafe

4 DECEMBER

28 days to go . . .

12:01 am

My hands were shaking as I held Rafe's rejected letter. *Dad* was the one who'd walked away from his relationship with Rafe? I couldn't believe it. I always thought Dad was the one who was being shut out, not the other way around.

I'd looked through Rafe's wedding photos pretty closely, and Dad had not been in any of them—he definitely wasn't standing by his twin as the best man. He must have ended up letting his brother down. Maybe that was why Rafe didn't look as happy as he should have . . . Dad must have found it too painful to be around his twin after the loss of one of his twin sons. It didn't make complete sense to me, but I knew from my experience that grief can do weird things to people. It can change them.

Like what was happening to Mum.

I refolded the letter and put it back in its envelope.

I thought again of all the things Rafe had done for us since Dad died. He'd given Mum a home when she was losing her own. He'd provided Gabbi with the best medical attention possible when she was in a coma, even changing the structure of his house for her. He'd taken Gabbi and Mum under his wing at a time when they needed protection most.

Maybe this was how involved in our family he'd wanted to be all along.

12:13 am

The coast was still clear outside, but I needed to get going. I figured Rafe would have made it to Marjorie's by now and would be back here any second.

I had a quick, final glance around the room and noticed Mum's red leather handbag on the floor near the dining table, its contents half-spilling out. She must have been really upset to have left that behind—it was usually glued to her.

Her bag seemed much heavier than it should have been. Inside was a bulging padded envelope. I pulled it out.

I couldn't believe what I was seeing printed on the top left-hand corner of the large envelope. "Rathbone and Associates."

What?

My head was spinning. What was Mum doing with a thick, bulky envelope from Sheldrake Rathbone?

There had to be an innocent explanation. *Right?*

The sound of a car in the street snapped me into action. I pocketed Dad's unread letter, shoved the heavy envelope from Mum's bag into my backpack and bolted out the back door.

Sure enough, Rafe had returned. He'd just pulled up in the driveway, and already I could hear Gabbi's voice as she climbed out of the car alongside Mum.

While they trundled into the house, I ran out onto the road.

As my feet pounded the ground on my way to Memorial Park, my thoughts whirled like a tornado: *Dad* had been responsible for the split from Rafe, not the other way around, and now it seemed as if Mum had been dealing with Rathbone. What was going on? Everything I thought I knew had been turned upside down.

Cenotaph
Memorial Park

1:12 am

Boges and Winter emerged from the shadows as I

ran up the steps and into the circular enclosure, where dead leaves skittered over the mosaic floor.

The moon was shining brilliantly through the stained glass window above, and the Ormond Angel seemed to look down on us sternly.

"What is it?" Winter asked. "You're so pale."

"It's just the moonlight," I replied. "Let's sit down," I suggested, as the pair scrutinized my face.

After I'd filled them in on my trip to Dolphin Point, I handed them Dad's unread letter from Rafe. They both skimmed over it eagerly.

"Rafe was telling the truth," said Boges. "He and your dad *were* really close until . . ."

". . . until the kidnapping," Winter whispered.

"I didn't see that coming," added Boges.

"Me neither," I said, pulling the padded envelope out of my backpack. "This is what I found in my mum's bag."

Winter eyed it closely.

"Well, go on," she said. "Open it!"

I did so reluctantly, afraid of what I was about to find. Boges and Winter jostled around me to see.

I tipped the contents out.

None of us could speak at first.

It wasn't a fat wad of documents. There,

gleaming in the moonlight beneath the radiant Angel above us, glowed the Ormond Jewel on top of the Ormond Riddle!

Winter took the Jewel in her hand. "*Amor et suevre tosjors celer,*" she whispered eerily, reciting the inscription inside as her forefinger traced the almost invisible letters. "A love whose works must always be kept secret." She looked up at me and asked the question that was in all of our minds. "Why would *your mum* have these?"

I could see my own shocked expression mirrored on the faces of Boges and Winter. We should have felt fantastic. We should have felt like leaping over the cenotaph in a single bound. Instead, dark questions had taken over.

"Your mum?" Boges asked slowly. "Your mum is Deep Water or Double Trouble?"

"It can't be right." I shook my head, refusing to accept it. "There must be an explanation."

"That scent that you almost identified back there at the undertakers'. . . Maybe you're repressing the memory," Boges continued, hinting at my reaction to the scent of Mum's perfume the last time we snuck into Rafe's house. "Maybe you know exactly who it belongs to, but you can't bear to face the truth, and that's why you can't bring yourself to recall it. It's your heart stopping you." Boges shook his head and ran his hands through his hair. "I can't believe your mum is *in* on this. . . Mrs. O," he said, in disbelief.

"Hang on a minute," I said defensively. "You don't know that's true. She could—"

"Oh, wow! What is that?" a voice interrupted us.

I swung around.

"What are you doing here, Gabbi?"

"You said you were coming here, so as soon as Uncle Rafe and Mum went to bed, I snuck out. Don't worry, they don't have a clue I'm gone!"

My little sister didn't look the least bit sorry about breaking the rules. In fact, she looked pretty proud of herself for wandering out alone to find me.

She'd been *kidnapped* before, but I didn't have the heart to tell her off, especially not right now when I was sick with suspicions about Mum.

She ran over to hug Boges and Winter.

"That's the Ormond Jewel," I said, finally answering Gabbi's question, "and that is the Ormond Riddle. These are the two things everyone's been after."

"Where did you find them?" she asked.

Winter looked down, avoiding the question, and fiddled with the laces on her sneakers, while Boges remained stunned, the two frown lines on his forehead forging together in a deep trough.

"Is that a real emerald?" she said, coming closer.

"You bet," Boges replied, finally speaking up for all of us. "It's the real thing. 'Big as a pigeon's egg,'" he quoted.

While Gabbi and Boges talked, Winter pulled me aside against the dark, curving wall of the cenotaph.

"Your *mum* had these? From Rathbone? In her bag?" she whispered, her worried eyes searching mine.

I nodded.

"*Mum* had them?" asked Gabbi, swinging around from Boges. "How come Mum had these things if everyone's been after them? I thought you said she didn't know anything about this."

I was lost for words. As I shrugged my shoulders, things seemed to slowly come into place. My mum must have always known more than she'd let on. After all, she'd seen the tracing paper and the empty jewel box, and she'd heard Rafe questioning me about the Ormond Riddle—she'd been there all along. I recalled her staring at Dad's drawing of the Angel up on my bedroom wall, before this mess began . . .

The cenotaph started to spin around me like I was trapped inside one of those anti-gravity carnival rides. *Mum?* Could Mum have been the person who—I tried to stop my brain from going there, but it was determined. My mum had been acting like a stranger to me almost all year. If she was capable of turning her back on her son, could she also have been capable of . . . attacking me? Locking me in a coffin and leaving me to die underground?

"Somebody say something!" cried Gabbi, walking over to me and tugging on my jacket. She slipped her hands into my pockets, and I brushed her away.

"My hands are cold," she whined. "What's wrong with you guys?"

"There has to be an explanation," I said.

"*Hello*?" said Gabbi. "Am I invisible? Why are you ignoring me?"

"Sorry, Gabs," said Boges. "We're just a little distracted right now with some new . . . umm . . . developments. Look, Cal," he said. "Let's just focus on the fact that we have them back. That's *good* news. Let's worry about the other things later, huh?"

"Boges is right," said Winter, with an arm around Gabbi. "There could be a perfectly reasonable explanation."

She hugged my sister, who was turning the Jewel over in her hands.

"We'd better get you back home," said Boges, tugging on one of Gabbi's braids.

My sister groaned and brushed Boges away.

"I can *help* you guys," she said. "I'm not a kid anymore. Why can't you see that?"

"We know," said Winter, "but it's just too dangerous right now. You need to stay home . . . and keep an eye on your mum and Rafe. We need someone to make sure they're OK. OK?"

"Let's go," said Boges, to Gab. "I'll walk you home."

Treehouse

3:00 am

Back at the treehouse I charged up my phone and realized I had a couple of missed calls from Sharkey. Winter and I listened carefully to his voicemail message, hoping for news on our trip.

"Cal, it's Nelson," he'd said. "I have the tickets. The four of us are booked to fly out on the twenty-third. Do yourselves a favor and stay out of strife until then."

"Wow, it's all happening!" said Winter excitedly. "Can you believe we finally have a date, plus the Jewel and the Riddle in our possession?"

"Crazy stuff," I said, relieved, but unable to shake off the bad feelings I had about Mum.

A tiny spider crawled up Winter's arm. She yawned and shook it off gently.

"Until we fly out, I'm going to have to find better

accommodation, Cal. A girl like me can only live up a tree for so long. I might give Sharkey a buzz back and see if he can hook me up with a place to stay. Somewhere Sligo will never find me."

9 DECEMBER

23 days to go . . .

Fit For Life

4:40 pm

Boges, Winter and I sat on upturned crates out in back of the gym. We were meeting up with Sharkey to go over our travel plans, and we were waiting for him to return from the showers.

I'd missed Winter's company in the last few days. Sharkey had set her up in a motel that was run by a retired cop he knew. She'd tried to convince me to join her there, but I felt safer up in the tree on Luke Lovett's property. I also didn't want to risk bringing any attention to her. We couldn't let Sligo find her.

"I have something for you," said Boges proudly. He passed me some sort of diving watch. "It works like a regular watch, but it's also a radio beacon."

"Another distress beacon?"

"Yep. Consider it an early Christmas present.

I've adapted the winder so that if you press it like so," Boges leaned over and depressed the tiny button, which lit the watch face up with a strange, blue pulsing light, "you'll activate the emergency radio signal. I have the receiver here," he said, holding out a similar watch on his wrist. "This watch picks up the signal and gives me the GPS coordinates of where you are."

I tightened the watch around my wrist, while Winter shuffled forward to get a closer look at it.

"Awesome, Boges," she said. "Hopefully he won't need to use it like last time."

"Better safe than sorry," he said. "I was hoping it would soften some other news I have," Boges began.

I groaned. "Spit it out."

"I read a report online this morning that the authorities believe you're a flight risk."

"A flight risk? How do they know?"

"I'm not sure, but they're upping security at all the major airports until you're detained."

"They'll have to catch you first," said Winter.

"OK," said Sharkey, stepping out of the back door with a clap of his hands. He pulled a crate over to us and sat down on it. His dark hair was wet and slicked back. "I figured it would be a good idea to make a basic plan and start getting used to our stories ahead of time. So here's the deal. We're traveling as a school group, OK? I'm your teacher."

"Cool," said Boges. "Our history teacher? You kinda look like you could be a history teacher."

"Suits me," Sharkey replied. "I suggest we all drive together to the airport. I'm happy to leave my car in one of the parking lots. You'll be safer, Cal, as part of a group. Have you heard about the airport alerts?"

"Boges just told me."

"The authorities will be on the alert for an individual, not a group."

"We might be traveling as a group," I said, "but everyone still has to go through security as an individual. . . I hope I make it through OK."

"Yeah, I'm not so sure I'll be OK either," said Boges. "I'm known to the police, as they say. I could be on their radar. Do you think they'll pull *me* out?" he asked Sharkey. "Do you think my name's on some sort of watch list?"

"Won't be a problem," he replied, patting Boges on the shoulder.

"How can you be so sure?" Boges asked, puzzled.

Sharkey dug into his gym bag and pulled out a brown paper bag. He tossed it to Boges.

"What's this?" asked Boges, as he pulled out a dark blue passport.

"Open it."

Boges leafed through the pages. "Hey, that's my picture! *Joshua Stern*?" he read.

"That's your new name, buddy," said Sharkey.

Boges started shaking his head. "Nelson," he said, with a worried look, "this would be great, but it was hard enough us getting the money together for Cal's passport and our tickets. We don't have enough left over for this one."

"Don't worry about the money," said Nelson. "I bargained with the forger and convinced him to do another two for me."

"Two?" I asked.

Sharkey promptly produced another brown bag and tossed it to Winter.

Winter caught it with the excitement of a kid at Christmas.

"Grace Lee?" she read.

"That's right," said Sharkey. "With Vulkan Sligo's connections, we don't want your name alerting the authorities to our presence at the airport, either."

I reached out to shake Sharkey's hand. "Thanks so much," I told him. "You must have done some sweet talking to get three passports for us. Ireland would be nothing but a pipe dream if we didn't have you to help us out."

"Forget about it. The thing you guys really need to do now," he said, "is to practice your new names until you respond to them just like you do to your real names. Like you, Matt Marlow," he added, eyeballing me.

"Yes, sir," I said. "Maybe you could all call me Matt from now on?"

"Sure thing, Matty," said Winter.

"Thanks, Grace. You too, Josh," I added.

"No problem, Matt," Boges replied.

"Good," said Sharkey. "Our departure date's going to come around fast. In the meantime, get to know the details on your passports and start packing. I'll hold onto the tickets for now, and I'll call you to organize another meeting soon."

"Sharkey," said Boges, "is it OK if I give my mum your number to call—she's a bit concerned about this 'study trip' occurring over Christmas. Can you just tell her it's legit?"

Sharkey looked at Boges sternly and pursed his lips. "I don't like lying, but I'll do it."

13 DECEMBER

19 days to go . . .

Outside Ryan Spencer's apartment

8:10 am

Ryan had been on my mind for days, and this morning I was drawn to his place like a magnet, as though I had to see him and start making up for lost time. I think it was all the photos of Dad and Rafe I'd been mulling over that made me want to speak to *my* twin.

Even though I hardly knew him, he was the only family member I felt safe seeking out, and he deserved to know everything *I* now knew about our history.

I had no simple way of getting in touch with him, so I had no choice but to linger outside his apartment building, hoping he'd show up sooner or later. I leaned against the fence, reading a copy of yesterday's newspaper that I'd found in a nearby recycling pile.

It was a hot December morning, and if it

hadn't been for the questions squirming around in my mind concerning my mum, I would have felt great about getting closer and closer to our goal in Ireland.

"Good morning, Ryan," said an old lady, passing by the mailboxes.

I looked up, startled, realizing she'd mistaken me for my brother.

"Hi," I answered, flustered, hoping she'd be happy with that and move on.

"How's your dear mother?" she continued.

"She's good, thanks," I replied, as plainly as I could, silently begging her to leave me alone.

"Be a pet and tell her I said hello," she added, before finally shuffling along to the building next door.

I breathed a huge sigh of relief, just as a familiar figure appeared at the door to the building.

"Ryan!" I called out.

I hurried across to him, and his face lit up when he saw me.

"Hey!" he said. "I wanted to get in touch with you, but I didn't know how. Quick, come upstairs."

"I don't want to freak your mum out again," I said cautiously, thinking about how the last time I'd been here I'd left him behind with his mum— the woman who'd adopted him—lying unconscious on the floor.

"She's not here—already left for work. The place is empty."

"So you don't have to be somewhere?"

"Nowhere that can't wait."

8:42 am

Ryan hunched across from me, listening intently over the coffee table in his living room. I tried to tell him everything I possibly could about us, and I tried to answer all of his questions about *his* mum and whether she knew who he really was.

"We were abducted?" Ryan asked, his eyes searching my face.

"Yes."

"And my mum—I mean, my *adoptive* mum—had no idea of who I really was? That I was the missing baby, Samuel?"

"That's right."

After I'd passed on everything I knew, Ryan was silent for a long time. I wondered what was going through his mind—was he angry? Upset? He stood up and went to the window, looking out across the rooftop where I'd once chased him.

Finally, he turned to me and said, "This explains something I've thought about for as long as I can remember—that something wasn't quite right with me, not right with my family.

174

I've never really fit in. I don't look like my mum, and we're both really different people. I've always had this nagging feeling that something . . ."

"Something was missing?" I finished for him.

He nodded. "I've always had this dream too," he began, "which is finally starting to make sense. I'm in this cold, dark place, crying, then all of a sudden I'm somewhere else, but wanting to go back. . . It must have been about you," he said. "You were left behind in that building."

Goose bumps crawled across the skin on my forearms. The incident had haunted his dreams too.

"But why did Murray Durham want to do away with us?" asked Ryan. "I don't get it."

I shook my head. "He was just carrying out orders."

"From who?"

"I don't know. Durham didn't know either."

"Cal, I want to ask a favor."

"Go on."

"I really want to speak to your mum. I mean *our* mum." He pulled out his phone. "I just want to talk to her. Tell her I'm OK. Will you call her for me?"

I thought about it for a second. There were so many reasons why I should have said no. Including my suspicions about her involvement in the DMO. But this was her missing child. Maybe she'd listen to him.

"Here, use my phone," said Ryan, handing his cell to me. He looked so hopeful, nervous and brave.

"That's OK," I said, turning down his phone. "I'll use mine." I stopped thinking about it, pulled out my phone and just dialed her number.

"It's ringing," I said, already starting to have second thoughts. Could I make things worse and put Ryan in danger? But he wasn't the heir— *I* was the first-born son. *I'd* beaten him into the world. I hoped that meant he was safe.

Before I could decide, she answered.

"Hello?"

I took a deep breath. "Mum," I said. "It's me. Don't hang up. Just hear me out. I have Ryan Spencer with me. My twin brother. *Samuel*, Mum."

I waited for her to say something, but she didn't.

"He's here, and he'd really like to talk to you," I added.

"Cal, please leave Samuel's memory alone. He's dead and gone—" her voice choked on a sob. "Why are you torturing me like this?"

"But Mum, he's here! I promise I'm not lying! Please, at least talk to him?"

"I can't, Cal. I just can't. I have to go."

The line went dead. I felt a mixture of pain and fury spin through me. She didn't want to listen.

I looked over at Ryan. "No good, huh?" he asked.

I shook my head.

He looked pretty disappointed, but he quickly shrugged it off. "She'll come around sooner or later," he said, with conviction. "Especially when we meet face-to-face."

I couldn't imagine that happening with Mum acting the way she was, but I kept my mouth shut.

"I'd better go," I said. "I have lots to do before I—" I hesitated, unsure about whether I should mention my Ireland plans.

"Before you what?" he asked curiously. "You can trust me, you know. I am your brother, after all. We have at least fifteen years' worth of helping each other out of trouble to catch up on. You can count on me."

In this new world of not being able to trust anyone, even those closest to me, I was surprised I believed him.

"I'm flying out," I explained. "Going to Ireland—leaving in the afternoon of the twenty-third."

"How come? Won't that be dangerous? Aren't you worried you'll be caught, going to an airport? Isn't that a bit—"

"Stupid?" I interrupted. "Possibly, but I just have to risk it. If I can make it to Ireland, there's a chance I can clear my name. I have to take that chance. I have a fake passport, and I'm hoping that's enough. I have no alternative, and time's running out."

"No alternative, eh?" he said, giving me a long, hard look. "I guess I should say good luck."

"Thanks," I said.

We exchanged phone numbers, said goodbye, and I headed back to the treehouse.

18 DECEMBER

14 days to go . . .

Treehouse

4:36 pm

Our plane to Ireland was leaving in less than a week, so Boges, Winter and I were poring over everything we had so far on the DMO, in preparation.

I spread everything out on the floor as best I could, while Winter wrote up a quick list.

"The first thing we need to do when we get there," announced Winter, as she handed me her list, "is set up a meeting with the Keeper of Rare Books at Trinity College in Dublin. We play it low-key—we don't want to reveal everything we know—we just want to find out what he can offer us. If he can help us find the missing two lines from the Riddle, we'll be way ahead of the game."

Boges and I must have looked unconvinced.

DRAWINGS

Angel – Ormond Angel, Piers Ormond

Butler with blackjack – Black Tom Butler, the tenth Earl of Ormond and Queen Elizabeth's agent in Ireland. Given the OJ by QE1.

Things that can be worn – the Ormond Jewel

Collared monkey with ball – painting of Queen Elizabeth?

Sphinx and Roman bust – Ormond Riddle . . . and Caesar shift?

Boy with rose – Ormond Singularity heir? Tudor rose?

Door with number '5' – link to photos from memory stick?

Kilfane & G'managh transparency – a map?

ORMOND JEWEL & ORMOND RIDDLE –

double-key code link to Ormond Singularity.

PHOTOS FROM MEMORY STICK

Castle ruins

Gate with number '5' in it – link to wardrobe/door drawing?

Carved wardrobe – same as above

"I don't care what contacts and resources Rathbone, or even Sligo have," Winter scoffed. "That doesn't mean they'll beat us." She flicked her hair back from her face before speaking again. "Then, depending on how our meeting with the Keeper goes, I think we should head to the place your dad was staying in—the Clonmel Way Guest House in Carrick-on-Suir. Boges, I mean, *Josh*, did you bring the map of Ireland you printed out?"

"Sure did, *Grace*," he said, unfolding a huge map and spreading it out over the top of the papers on the floor. The three of us peered over it, examining it closely.

"Carrick-on-Suir is some way from Dublin," said Winter, "but not so far by bus or train."

"As soon as we reach the guesthouse, we should start searching the area. Maybe a local will recognize this." I pulled out a photo of the castle ruins.

"And remember," said Boges, "we'll be traveling in an Irish winter. It could be snowing, so pack plenty of warm gear." With that he pulled out a blue-and-white striped beanie and tugged it on his head. It entirely covered his curly hair, which was slowly growing back after Winter had shaved it.

I looked up from the tracing paper. "There's so much we still don't know. That black dot could be pointing out nothing but a good place to grab lunch."

"That would be good too, but not exactly what we were hoping for." Boges laughed and started packing up his gear. "I'm off to meet Nelson now, just to go over the final details. Wow, you guys," he said, a broad smile stretching across his face, "can you believe this is all really happening? We're actually going to Ireland!"

"It *is* pretty awesome," agreed Winter, a smile growing across her lips too. "I'm excited. It's going to be one huge adventure, no matter what happens."

"You're right, guys," I said, starting to feel the enthusiasm building. "I guess I'll see you both next week—ready and raring to go!"

6:10 pm

As soon as I was alone again, my nerves resurfaced. Every time thoughts of my mum crept into my mind, I tried to push them away and focus on going to Ireland. Whenever thoughts of being captured at the airport before even setting foot on the plane snuck in, I'd wipe them out by imagining the exhilaration I knew I would feel as soon as I was finally on my way.

23 DECEMBER

9 days to go . . .

11:00 am

Outside the treehouse window, the sun was shining. The birds in a tree nearby were squawking so loudly that I could hardly hear Winter's voice on the phone.

"Speak up," I told her.

"I'm all ready," she said louder, her voice trembling with excitement. "Nelson's picking up *Josh* first, then me, then we're coming over to get you. He'll be here at the motel any minute. . . . I hate to say it, but I'm feeling pretty nervous. What if something goes wrong?"

"We can't let it," I said, even though I was feeling just as freaked out by what we were about to do.

11:21 am

As I waited, I checked and re-checked my backpack, anxiously making sure I had everything I needed. We were supposed to be at the airport by one o'clock for our flight at three. I combed my hands through my hair, styling it forward so that it hung across my face, almost covering my eyes.

The contacts! I'd almost forgotten about the dark contacts Winter had given me. I quickly dug them out of my bag and blinked madly as I put them in.

11:29 am

When I heard Sharkey's car pulling up in the alley behind the back fence, I checked that the coast was clear, then clambered down the treehouse rope and snuck out of the Lovetts' yard for the last time.

"Good morning, sir," I joked, as I climbed into the car.

Sharkey laughed awkwardly, making me feel even more nervous than I already was. I looked around the car at my friends—everyone looked really uneasy.

"What's wrong?" I asked. "I mean, apart from the obvious—the fact that you're a phony school group helping the notorious Psycho Kid escape the country."

"Sharkey just told us some bad news," replied Boges.

"There's a huge security convention happening

over the next four days," explained Sharkey, as we headed for the airport. "Counter-terrorism squads from all over the world have descended on the city. They'll be practicing maneuvers—raiding buildings, securing roads and bridges, locking down the airport, that sort of thing."

"Locking down the airport?" I asked, recalling what Eric Blair had told me about Strike Force Predator.

"The airports were already on high alert, but now security has tripled," Sharkey continued. "Random stop-and-search exercises of cars and public transportation will be carried out, I heard."

Boges shook his head. "It gets worse. The police commissioner has said that instead of this exercise being a sterile operation, they're giving the program real focus by having your capture as part of the agenda. Apparently the authorities are even going to be doing a bit of random fingerprinting at Departures."

"What do we do?"

"Nothing we *can* do," replied Sharkey. "We've just gotta do everything we planned and hope we slip through somehow."

I exhaled loudly and stared through the window at the fast-moving world outside.

"Come on," Winter comforted me, patting my

knee like my mum used to. "Somehow we'll get through. I can feel it."

I turned to her and forced a smile. She was wearing an emerald-green beret, and her dark hair tumbled down over her shoulders. I hoped her feeling was right.

"Do you all have your stories straight?" Sharkey asked.

"Absolutely," I replied, happy to have something to distract me from the somersaults in my stomach. "I'm Matt Marlow, traveling to Ireland with my friends Joshua Stern and Grace Lee, and our history teacher Mr. Nelson Sharkey."

Sharkey nodded, but I could see that even he was nervous. He was used to being the law-abiding good guy, and now he was aiding and abetting a wanted fugitive.

The number of police cars on the street, and helicopters in the sky, grew thicker the closer we came to the airport. Luckily the lane leading to Departures that the police had taken over for random checking was full as we cruised past.

12:25 pm

Sharkey parked, and we all began the nail-biting trek inside. I stopped myself from looking around, but I couldn't control the sweat that had broken out on my forehead. I knew the people on passport control were trained to look for suspicious characters, and if I didn't control my anxious, darting glances and do something about the sweating, I'd be discovered.

With Christmas so near, the whole airport was buzzing. I guessed most travelers were going on holidays, maybe joining their families overseas, like Sharkey. They were fussing over luggage labels, chasing kids around, wheeling suitcases that were probably weighed down with presents. I felt like our somber group was sticking out like a sore thumb.

For me, this was the first part of the final obstacle in this year-long quest. I could almost taste victory. I shifted the weight of my backpack. Inside I had the warm clothes Boges had lent me for the Irish winter, and beneath them was a smaller, zip-lock bag containing the Riddle, the Jewel and our notes. I wasn't checking my backpack in—nothing was going to separate me from everything I had inside.

"Just relax, Matt," said Winter, who had obviously noticed the state I was in.

"I'm trying, *Grace*," I said, through gritted teeth.

"OK," Nelson interrupted. "We have our stories straight, so let's check in. Any questions, just refer to me."

I looked up and noticed that Sharkey had beads of sweat on his brow. He seemed really nervous for me; his eyes were scanning the international check-in area.

We just had to make it onto the plane.

1:21 pm

The four of us had made it through check-in—our fake passports had held up so far—and we were following Sharkey, walking over to the line for passport control. None of us had said anything to each other since checking in—we were all too tense.

Suddenly Sharkey slowed up, forcing us to stop abruptly behind him. He casually turned around to us, but the look on his face was more than unsettling.

I quickly peered past him, and a feeling of horror took over as I realized we were walking towards the security convention's fingerprinting station.

"What do we do?" Winter whispered.

Sharkey looked stumped for a second.

"Just walk on by as confidently as you can," he eventually instructed, while pretending to look for something in his wallet. "There's no turning back for us now. We're just a school group, remember? Hopefully they won't pick us out and call us over. If they *do* call us over, then I guess we'd all better start praying for a miracle."

My heart was beating out of my chest as Sharkey turned around and continued walking. My two friends and I had no choice but to follow.

"Excuse me, sir," a voice called out from the security station. "Would you and your group please step over here for a random fingerprint test?"

Those words winded me like a punch in the gut. The kind of punch that sends you crashing to the ground. The kind of punch that you don't recover from.

I panicked, looking at Boges and Winter frantically. They looked as petrified as me.

Sharkey turned to us once more, and I felt sick. "Come along, kids," he said to us, but I could see in his saddened eyes that he knew our quest was over. We were about to have our fingerprints taken, and that meant the police had won. They were about to capture their target.

We'd failed. Solving the DMO just wasn't meant to happen.

I closed my eyes and thought of the life I wanted to have—the normal life with Mum, Gabbi, Rafe and my twin. The life I imagined was about to be irrevocably lost.

A rapid change in the energy of the crowd suddenly washed over us. The row of police and security guards at the fingerprinting station ahead abruptly dismantled. Officers stood up from their posts and rushed over to a TV screen. Others nearby reached for their walkie-talkies.

What was happening?

My heart was thumping in my throat as my eyes darted around again, trying to make sense of the commotion. Had they locked onto me through the surveillance cameras? Was a riot squad about to tackle me?

Where could I hide? Where could I go? I was trapped!

I spun around. The whole airport erupted into chaos. Travelers were dropping their bags and rushing to catch a glimpse of the airport TV screens, talking and gesturing excitedly to each other.

What was happening?

"Look!" cried Winter, pointing to a smaller screen in the quarantine area.

The four of us squinted up at the screen. It was a news report. A breaking news banner ran beneath the newscaster.

"'Teen fugitive, Callum Ormond,'" I read, 'leads police on wild chase. Police Commissioner calls for calm.'"

Winter grabbed my arm.

"We interrupt this broadcast for breaking news," the newscaster announced. I strained my ears to hear her words over the hubbub around me. "We're going live to our on-the-scene reporter. Tell us, Anton, we've had reports that Callum Ormond has been located and is leading police on a *car* chase? Where is he, and what is happening as we speak?"

"It's a baffling scene here, Julia. It appears that shortly after two o'clock this afternoon, wanted fugitive Callum Ormond rammed a car into the doors of the city police headquarters. He then jumped out and fled *on foot*, and he was captured just moments ago outside the Town Hall. The entire incident was caught on closed-circuit TV, and police have confirmed that they have arrested Ormond and that he has been taken into custody."

What?

Boges, Winter and Sharkey stood rooted beside me, staring at the screen.

"What on earth is going on?" hissed Boges. "They've arrested Callum Ormond? But—"

"*Ryan!*" I cried softly, with unspeakable relief. "Ryan must be behind this! He knew I was flying out today! He's done this to make sure I get out of the country!"

Overhead, we could hear the helicopters that were hovering near the airport move away, flying towards the city.

The officer who had called us over earlier waved us on hurriedly. "We'd better make our move right now," said Sharkey, confidence returning to his eyes.

He beamed as he led us towards the distracted customs counter. He knew we were safe. No one would be looking for me now.

2:32 pm

We'd made it. The four of us slumped into the stiff chairs of the departure lounge, exhausted, drained, relieved. We'd be on the plane within minutes.

I pulled out my phone, preparing to switch it off, when I noticed an unread message sitting in my inbox from about an hour ago.

📱 cal, it's ryan. i'm about to do something pretty crazy . . . i really hope it helps u make it through the airport & onto that plane. who knows, it may even force our mother into seeing me. hopefully the cops believe me when i tell them it's just an innocent driving lesson gone wrong! safe trip, bro! see u when u get back!

24 DECEMBER

8 days to go . . .

Temple Inn
Dublin

7:26 pm

The freezing-cold air of Christmas Eve was a shock, even though we'd anticipated it. We hailed a taxi to take us to our small hotel in Temple Bar, in the southwest of Dublin. Christmas lights lined the riverside quays, and the driver commented on several points of interest, including the Liffey River, the Abbey Theater and the blue lights of the Garda—police—Station. We were too exhausted to pay much attention, although it was good to know that the Garda wouldn't be looking out for the Psycho Kid.

At the hotel, we all checked in under our fake names. Boges and I were sharing a room, while Winter had a tiny attic room above us. She could barely turn around in there, but she was more than happy with it. Sharkey's room was just across the corridor from us. Other Sharkeys from all over the world had also arrived in Ireland for their huge Christmas reunion. Their celebrations were starting tomorrow, at a place called Roscommon, so Nelson was only staying one night. In the morning he would be heading off, then meeting up with us again after a few days.

9:00 pm

After we'd settled in, Boges and I called Dr. Theophilus Brinsley, the Keeper of Rare Books, to let him know we'd arrived.

"Tomorrow's Christmas Day," he said. "How about we meet on Boxing Day? The library will be quiet because of the holiday. Meet me outside on the stairs at ten o'clock."

"Perfect. See you soon. Oh, and Merry Christmas," I added, before hanging up.

I looked over to Boges. He'd already collapsed back into his bed, snoring softly. I wanted to do exactly that too—sleep. On a bed. A *bed*. With sheets and a pillow and a clean pillowcase. For the first time in almost a year, I felt safe enough to sleep soundly.

Before I drifted off, I pictured my dad. I shoved all of my recent suspicions and uncertainties out of my mind and visualized him as I remembered him on the day he left for Ireland. Being here, I was feeling closer to him than ever. Soon I would go to Clonmel Way Guest House and retrace his last known steps.

25 DECEMBER

7 days to go . . .

10:15 am

The breakfast room was festooned with colored lights, and two wooden reindeer stood by the entrance—their antlers decorated with shiny baubles hanging on golden threads. We were the only people in there.

Sharkey had shared a quick cup of coffee with us before leaving to go and meet his relatives for lunch. He'd looked a bit unsettled, and I guessed it was because he was missing his kids. Boges too, was looking a bit down. He'd called his mum and gran earlier, but he had never been happy about leaving them alone at Christmas.

"As soon as we get back home, we'll have to have our own Christmas lunch together. With lots of presents and a big roast with lots of potatoes," I said wishfully.

"Can't wait," said Winter.

"Me neither," said Boges, "especially for the feed."

Past Christmases with Mum and Dad had always made me and Gab think about how lucky we were. I knew Gabbi would be missing me today, but I wondered how my mum felt and whether she'd met Ryan—her lost son—yet. Then I looked at this amazing girl across from me now, Winter, who'd lost so much and yet had such fierce determination to recover what was rightfully hers, while also helping me recover what was rightfully mine. I then turned to Boges, my loyal mate and ally. He was as solid as a rock.

"What's this?" asked Winter, picking up a small white envelope from the table, left where Sharkey had been sitting.

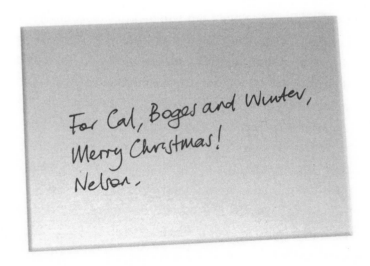

For Cal, Boges and Winter,
Merry Christmas!
Nelson.

"Open it," I urged.

Winter carefully eased it open, and out slipped a small plastic sleeve, the size of a credit card. Inside was a flat-pressed, four-leaf clover.

"How sweet," exclaimed Winter, holding it up for us to see. "He must have been too shy to just give it to us, so he left it behind. I hope it really is lucky!"

"That's cool," said Boges, examining it closely.

I looked down at the clover Sharkey had left behind. He was doing for us what I was sure he wished he could do for his own kids. Maybe I could somehow help reunite him with them once we were back home.

11:45 am

We'd decided to check out the location of tomorrow's meeting with the Keeper of Rare Books, so we bundled up and headed out into a bleak Christmas morning. We strolled along the cobbled streets, past pubs and convenience stores, following the map the hotel owner had given us for Trinity College.

Winter walked briskly beside me, wearing a long white coat and a red wool scarf tied around her neck. The green beret sat crookedly on her head, and she tugged on it to straighten it. Boges and I were both wearing long, black wool trench coats and beanies.

Being in Ireland, so far away from home, had definitely made me relax more than usual, but I was still very aware that Sheldrake Rathbone could be anywhere.

Trinity College
Dublin

12:00 pm

Church bells chimed as we walked through the quiet streets and through the huge Trinity College gateway. On the other side was an almost-deserted courtyard, dominated by a bell tower in the middle of the large, open square, surrounded by grand buildings. Only a few people, heads buried in their collars against the cold air, crossed the pathways through the perfect lawns. We paused at the bell tower and then followed the sign pointing towards the old library.

Standing on the steps outside, shivering in the cold, we smiled at each other. It was finally happening, after all these months. We'd made it to Ireland, and we were almost ready to take the prize. By tomorrow afternoon we could have the last two lines of the Ormond Riddle, and maybe we'd even know the location of the ruins in the photos Dad had taken. We could be way ahead of Rathbone in just twenty-four hours.

26 DECEMBER

6 days to go . . .

Trinity College
Dublin

9:55 am

Dr. Brinsley was a tall man with wispy white hair, a deeply furrowed brow and unusual half-moon glasses perched on his nose. He inspected the three of us over the top of his glasses with sharp, glittering eyes. We shook hands, and his glance fell on the Celtic ring I wore.

"Ah, it's nice to see an old classic. The Carrick bend," he said, with a light Irish accent, pointing to the angular Celtic pattern woven in the silver band. "Sometimes also called the Carrick knot. It's a popular design in the southeast of the country. So," he continued, "you're the infamous young man who's finally obtained the Ormond Riddle?"

I nodded, not sure how to respond.

"I must say, as much as I was hoping to meet you, I don't think I ever really expected to see

148

you here. It must have been exceptionally difficult to make it out of your country."

"Yes," I admitted.

"So you have the Riddle, but not the last two
lines, eh?"

"You said you could help me with those," I
reminded him, as we followed him through some
large double doors. I was really hoping I could
trust this guy.

"Yes, yes," he said, turning and closing the
double doors behind us. "Follow me, please."

He led us to the back offices of the library,
crowded with shelves that stood far too close to
each other, leaving only narrow passages between
them. It reminded me of Repro's old place. Once
through this maze we came to another door,
which he unlocked and ushered us through.

We were standing on a small landing with a
railing around it, similar to the dress circle of a
theater, overlooking the main body of the library
below. The gallery stretched away for hundreds of
yards, completely crammed with brown, leather-
clad books, sectioned into alcoves soaring up to
the cathedral-like ceiling.

"Wow," said Winter. "What a library! I've never
seen anything like it, except in movies."

"Coolest library ever," exclaimed Boges,
leaning over the railing beside me. "Look at all

those ancient books! There must be millions in here!"

"Not quite," said Dr. Brinsley. "We house over two hundred thousand antiquarian volumes, and the Book of Kells is just over there, in the Treasury building."

I didn't know what the "Book of Kells" was, but it must have been important.

"You have a treasure of your own," continued Brinsley, "which I am most anxious to see. Let's take a look at it, shall we?"

His eager eyes shone with greedy anticipation as he cleared some space on a nearby desk piled high with ancient books and papers. The Keeper of Rare Books removed some boxes from a bench and an armchair, then gestured to us to sit down before sitting behind the desk.

What if Brinsley had been waiting for this moment—a moment to seize our "treasure?" Any moment now he could draw a weapon and turn on us.

Or would Rathbone suddenly jump out from an alcove, demanding someone ring the Garda and waving extradition papers that would have me on the next flight back home to face arrest?

I couldn't tell if I was just being paranoid or cautious. With the stakes getting higher now that the end was so near, I didn't want to mess up now.

My friends and I sat down, and I carefully drew out the Ormond Riddle. I placed it on the Keeper's desk, just in front of me, my fingers firmly holding it in place as he leaned over it fervently.

"Ah! Here it is at last! The Ormond Riddle," he breathed. "We all thought it had been lost forever. Can it be true?" He snatched up a magnifying glass from a drawer and started scanning the medieval script.

Finally he straightened up, and his face was shining. His eyes looked watery with elation.

"All my life, ever since I was a little boy and first heard about the Ormond Singularity, I've wished that I could find the truth. My grandfather first told me about it. He'd heard about the legend from *his* grandfather. He'd grown up in Kilkenny, where it was rumored that the huge secret concerning the Ormond family was hidden in one of Black Tom's castles."

"Kilkenny?" I interrupted, thinking of Great-uncle Bartholomew's property in Mount Helicon. "Kilkenny" must have been an important place for him to name his home after it. I dug out one of Dad's ruin photos. "Is this a castle in Kilkenny? One of Black Tom's castles?"

Boges and Winter, who'd been keeping pretty quiet, both shot me wary glares.

Dr. Brinsley took the photo from me, looked at it and shook his head. "That's certainly not the famous Kilkenny Castle. Kilkenny Castle was saved from ruin and is open to the public—you should visit it. But this," he said, examining the photo, "is unfamiliar to me. These sorts of ruins are all over Ireland. It could be anywhere."

Kilkenny Castle definitely sounded like something we should check out, but my shoulders slumped. Finding the location in the photos was going to be much harder than we'd anticipated. I wondered how we could find out whether it was one of Black Tom's castles—one of the castles that could be hiding the secret of the Ormond Singularity.

He peered closer at the picture, picking up the magnifying glass again. "What's that figure there? Carved in the stones? That's very unusual for the times."

I stared hard and tried to make it out. I could almost see a figure cut into the stones of an upper turret, but I couldn't make out the detail. The angle of the photo made it almost impossible.

Dr. Brinsley straightened up and handed the photo back to me. "My grandfather also said that the Ormond Singularity gives passage to unimaginable treasure and wealth," he said, as though he were recalling an ancient myth. "As to the treasure trove," he continued, "you know how these stories grow over the centuries. Who knows what it really means?"

Unimaginable treasure and wealth. The phrase, so similar to my dad's, repeated itself in my mind. No wonder everyone was after it. Was that the secret that was hidden?

"Treasure?" asked Boges. "Do you believe there's some sort of buried treasure at one of Black Tom's castles?"

Dr. Brinsley shrugged. "Possibly. But the Ormond Singularity runs out in a matter of days. On December 31st, at midnight, to be exact. I happen to know that because I've been working on old titles and legal documents awaiting repeal. We have to find places here to house them all."

I looked around at the already over-stuffed shelves, desks and floor, and understood his problem.

"If something valuable—the treasure, so to speak—is found after that time," continued Dr. Brinsley, "it will all revert to the Crown. Which, of course, is where it is rumored to have originated."

"Let me get this straight," I said. "You're saying that the Ormond Singularity began with the Crown? With Queen Elizabeth the First and the Ormond family?" I asked him, careful not to

143

let on how much we knew already.

"It was something Queen Elizabeth granted to the Ormond family. Black Tom—the tenth Earl of Ormond—was her vice-regent here, protecting her interests against his Irish countrymen. He was the first Irishman to be given the Order of the Garter, and he wore it to bed every night."

"He wore it *to bed*?"

"That is so."

Winter nudged me. "Sounds like a serious crush to me," she whispered.

"But the Ormond Singularity is something much bigger than some decoration from the Queen," I said, thinking of the Ormond Jewel, "if you're talking about something like hidden treasure, here in Ireland."

My brain started turning around at those words. *Treasure . . . in Ireland.* Suddenly something made sense.

I turned to my friends. "Jennifer Smith said my dad had hurled a copy of Robert Louis Stevenson's *Treasure Island* across the room, frustrated that no one could understand what he was trying to say. He didn't want to *read* the book, he was trying to tell us about treasure *in* Ireland!"

"Your father knew something about this treasure trove?" Brinsley asked, frowning. "What else did he tell you?"

Immediately, I realized I'd said too much. "I don't know," I said, trying to brush it off. "He was so sick at the time, he was probably just hallucinating."

"That's right," Boges added, shaking his head. "Cal's dad died from an unknown virus that really messed with his head. He didn't know what he was saying."

I could see that Dr. Brinsley suspected we knew a great deal more than we were letting on. He turned his attention back to the Riddle on his desk.

"Sacrilege," he said, examining the clean cut across the bottom, "cutting off the last two lines."

"Yes," I agreed. "So you said you have information about the last two lines and where they could be?"

"First things first," he replied. "Do you also have the Ormond Jewel?"

I felt Boges kick my ankle, hard.

"It's in a safe," said Winter quickly. "Maybe we could arrange for you to have a look at it."

"May I ask how you came by it? My grandfather told me that there was once such a jewel, but that it had been lost generations ago. There had always been some connection between the Ormond

Riddle and the Jewel, he believed. Although what it might have been exactly, he did not know."

"It was recently acquired by my family," I said, reluctant to say that Dad had bought it while he was over here.

Dr. Brinsley squinted at me, as though willing me to hand over more information. "The Ormond Jewel—perhaps you could tell me what it looks like?"

Boges tentatively pulled out some photos of the Jewel and looked to me for approval to hand them over. I nodded to him.

"Here," he said, placing them in Brinsley's eager hands. There were four photos of the Jewel: one showing it closed, one showing it opened—revealing the portrait of Elizabeth the First inside, one showing the back with the rose and rosebud, while the last was a magnified depiction of the Middle French inscription.

After studying the photos for some time, Dr. Brinsley sat back and fanned himself with a wad of papers. "I must say," he said, "this is incredible. The usual explanation for this sort of precious, antiquarian item reappearing in modern day is that it has been held by a family for hundreds of years, so long that its origin and importance has been forgotten or lost, then the piece is sold when a family finds itself in financial difficulties. I'd say it came on the market fairly recently, was bought up by a dealer who also didn't know its history and then was sold for its face value—a jeweled miniature of Queen Elizabeth the First by an unknown artist. It would bring a high price just as it is, but certainly not the price it is actually worth."

The Keeper's face was filled with enthusiasm. "I think I'm starting to get some idea of what the Ormond Singularity might be. Mind you, it's only a guess—an educated guess—but there's something I have at home that I think you should see."

He pulled out a handkerchief and blew his nose, then leaned over to his desk and unlocked a drawer.

"In the meantime, I have this," he said, taking out a small document. It seemed to be written in Latin, but I could understand the date—1575. "It's a record of a marriage. The marriage of one of Black Tom's illegitimate sons, Piers Duiske Ormond—a secret marriage contracted at Duiske Abbey, Graignamanagh."

"G'managh? That's one of the names on the tracing paper," I said, swinging around to Boges. "Piers must have been a common name."

"This shows that Piers Duiske Ormond married a young lady called Anne Desmond," said the Keeper, "before he married the woman who is known to history as his wife, and with whom he had his son Edward."

I was confused. Too many names were being thrown around.

"Never mind all that," Dr. Brinsley said, as if reading my mind. "What *is* important is the record of this secret marriage. Especially since I suppose you already know that Black Tom outlived his legitimate heirs?"

"What's all this got to do with the Riddle and the Jewel, Dr. Brinsley?" I asked.

"It will make sense in good time, young man." He paused to take a sip of water from a mug on his desk. "Someone had hidden it in one of the ancient books that we bought from the Black Abbey some years ago."

Piers Ormond of the stained glass window had been at the Black Abbey. Had he hidden the original record of the secret wedding after copying it for his collection of papers? Had he been meaning to return and collect it when he had more information, before the war prevented his plan?

"Here," said the Keeper, "is the name of Piers Duiske Ormond's father, the tenth Earl of Ormond, Black Tom Butler. And here, where his mother's name *should* be, there's only this—" The Keeper adjusted his half-moon glasses and cleared his throat. "*Magna domina incognita*," he intoned in Latin.

"A great lady. Unnamed, unknown," Boges translated.

"Well done, young man. I see you know your Latin."

"But I still don't see what this has to do with anything," I said.

"It has *everything* to do with it. I've been studying the Singularity for years now. I don't have the whole picture by any means, but I have some information about it. Just now, seeing the photos of the Jewel, the text of the inscribed motto and what it implies . . . I can't help playing around with certain possibilities." He looked around suddenly, as if wary of his surroundings. "This place is too public for this sort of discussion. This may be even more dangerous than I first anticipated."

"Oh, it's a dangerous business," I assured him, considering the countless times in the last year I had come close to death. "No doubt about that."

Dr. Brinsley gestured towards us, urging us to lean in closer to hear what he had to say. "Please come to my house tomorrow evening," he whispered. "There's a sketch my grandfather did that I want to show you. After seeing the Jewel with its inscription, my instincts tell me that the sketch is of great importance. Perhaps you might be able to help? Especially when I tell you some thoughts I'm starting to entertain as a possibility, wild as they might be."

I'd come to Dublin to get answers, not a whole bunch of new questions. I directed the conversation back to basics.

"You told us you had information about the missing last two lines of the Ormond Riddle," I said again.

"Ah, yes," he said. "I *can* help you with that. Somewhat."

"Please tell us what you know," said Winter, her face eager. "That's what we're here for, after all."

"Those last two lines are believed to have been written by Black Tom himself." He looked at us as if waiting for a response. I didn't care who'd written them, I just wanted to *see* them, read them, apply the Caesar shift to them. Every instinct told me that the last two lines would deliver the secret of the Ormond Singularity to us.

"So do you have the last two lines or not?" urged Winter, clearly becoming as impatient as I was feeling.

"Not exactly, but I can tell you where I believe they are. In a copy of an antique book. Sir James Butler's *Lives of the Saints*."

"Is it here?" asked Boges, glancing over the

thousands of books shelved from floor to ceiling all the way along both sides of the immense expanse of the long gallery.

"I'm afraid it's not quite as simple as that," Brinsley replied. He raised his eyebrows before continuing. "As I told your friend who called last night—"

"*My friend who called last night*?" I repeated, frowning, looking around at the others. I was met with shocked silence. "None of us called last night," I said firmly. A cold chill ran through my bloodstream.

"No," said Boges. "None of us called you. Who do you mean? Who did you speak to about this?"

"You must be mistaken," said Dr. Brinsley, peering at me. "He knew all about *you*. Introduced himself to me and informed me of how he was here in Ireland helping you search for the meaning of the Ormond Singularity. He had an unusual first name, although his second name is common in Ireland—as a place name too."

I tensed up at the threat to us that this revelation implied. "There's a place in Ireland called 'Rathbone'?"

"'Rathbone?'" Dr. Brinsley repeated. "What does Rathbone have to do with it? No, the chap's name was Sligo. Vulkan Sligo. *County* Sligo's in the west coast province of Connacht."

Winter stiffened with fear beside me.

Vulkan Sligo was in Ireland!

"What did you tell him?" I demanded, jumping out of my chair and joining Boges and Winter who were already on their feet, ready to run.

Dr. Brinsley looked confused and concerned. "Just that I hoped I'd be seeing you today."

"You told him we'd be here?!" shrieked Winter. "What else did you tell him?"

"That you had the text of the Ormond Riddle," replied Brinsley, flustered. "He sounded a perfect gentleman."

"He's a notorious criminal!" shouted Winter. "He's tried to kill us! He wants Cal dead! Cal, we have to get out of here, now! He could be in here somewhere!" Her eyes darted around—she was petrified. Boges too, was wide-eyed and panicking, leaning over the railing, scanning the library for any sign of Sligo or one of his thugs.

"All right, let's go," I said to my friends. I stopped for a second to warn Brinsley. "Dr. Brinsley," I said, "I don't want to scare you, but you could be in great danger too. You must believe me. Vulkan Sligo has been trying get me out of the way—"

"—*kill* you," Winter interrupted, her face pale. "He's been trying to *kill* you, Cal." She turned to Dr. Brinsley. "He wants him out of the way so he can beat him to the Ormond Singularity."

The Keeper of Rare Books gave me a hard look that I couldn't interpret. Maybe he just didn't *want* to believe this.

"I said I would help you with the last two lines of the Ormond Riddle, and that offer still stands." Brinsley grabbed a pen and started scrawling an address on the back of an envelope. "Tomorrow I should be finished up here by eight. Come to my place at nine. Come through the back door. Here's my address," he added, handing me the envelope.

"Cal, we have to get out of here," Winter pleaded.

"I know, I know," I said. "Please, Dr. Brinsley," I begged him. "If you hear from Sligo again, please don't tell him you saw us here today. Don't tell him anything. Our lives depend on it."

He picked up the Ormond Riddle after I'd let go of it in a panic. I could see something in his face that looked like rabid hunger. Everyone who'd heard of this business seemed to want a piece of the action.

"I'd like that back now, please," I said, trying to sound casual and cool.

Dr. Brinsley flashed me a glinting smile. "You could always leave it with me until tomorrow evening . . ."

Boges stepped forward. "Not negotiable," he said, swiftly snatching up the Riddle.

With that, we ran back the way we'd come—swiftly weaving through the towers of books and mazes of shelving before quickly disappearing into the cold courtyard outside.

12:13 pm

Hands shoved deep in pockets, and wishing I'd worn a scarf like Winter, I walked nervously with the others around St. Stephen's Green. Bare trees raised their dark limbs to the white sky, and even the ducks on the half-frozen ponds looked chilly.

We were all frustrated and angry. The vague feeling of ease we'd experienced on arrival had been short-lived. I was just as on edge as I'd been back at home. In fact, I was worse. Time was ticking by, and now I was being hunted down in a foreign country.

My breath steamed in the air ahead of us as I spoke. "Dr. Brinsley just doesn't realize the danger surrounding the Ormond Singularity. He wasn't taking our warnings seriously enough." Something else was troubling me too. "What if Sligo's already swayed him?" I asked the others. "What if tomorrow night's meeting is a trap? We may have dodged Sligo today, but what if he's at Brinsley's place, waiting for us, at nine o'clock tomorrow?"

"It's a possibility that we have to be prepared for, dude," Boges replied. "It's a risk we have to take."

"What if Brinsley intends on stealing the Ormond Riddle for himself?" asked Winter. "Did you see the look on his face when he was examining it? He didn't want to hand it back once you let go, Cal."

"He sure didn't," said Boges. "It was like he realized something as we were sitting there. Like he saw something, understood something, that he wasn't quite ready to share just yet. Tomorrow night's going to be interesting."

4:05 pm

We spent the rest of the day trying to see as much of Dublin as we could, although we were pretty uneasy knowing that Sligo was in town. Winter fell in love with the wrought iron seahorses on the lampposts—cool horses with arched necks, their raised front legs ending in layered fins and muscular upper bodies tapering down into scaly, mermaid-like tails.

We were jumping at the sound of every passing car, and we constantly used counter-surveillance, taking sudden turns and doubling back on ourselves until we were hopelessly lost and had to pull out the map that we'd taken from the hotel.

It was impossible to relax. Eventually we decided it would be best to go back to the hotel. The thought of somewhere private and warm was too tempting.

Winter was really worried about Sligo tracking her down, but she hadn't checked in under her real name—none of us had—so we hoped that would keep her safe. For now.

27 DECEMBER

5 days to go . . .

Parnell Square

8:35 pm

We found the address Brinsley had given us in Parnell Square, north of the Liffey River. His place was a stone row house with a few steps leading up to the red front door. The brass door knocker, decorated with a green and red holly wreath, gleamed in the streetlight.

I took one last look around as we returned from checking out the alley that ran along the back of the row houses. There was no one around. Except for us, Parnell Square was deserted.

I made a quick call to Nelson Sharkey. I'd told him about the meeting over the phone last night.

"Nelson speaking," he said, and I could hear the sounds of people talking and laughing in the background.

"We're about to go inside," I said. "If anything goes wrong, you have his address."

"OK, got that. But I'm a few hours away, remember. Be very careful. You can't trust anyone. Are you sure you haven't been followed?"

"Pretty sure," I answered.

"Have you checked the rear of the property? Checked no one's watching the place?"

"Yep, we're cool."

"No sign of Sligo?"

"Nope. Anyway, it sounds like the party needs you. Call you later." I hung up and looked at my shivering friends. "Let's do it."

We walked back around to the alley at the rear of the house, went through the gate and knocked on the back door.

"Dr. Brinsley?" I called out, after a minute or two.

The door wasn't locked, and with the slightest push, it swung open. The three of us wandered inside and looked around. Several closed, wood-paneled doors led off from the black-and-white marble-floored square we'd walked into, and I could see a staircase leading to the upper floor.

"Dr. Brinsley?" I called again, as our shoes tapped along the floor.

"I don't like this," said Boges. "Something feels wrong."

I felt Winter shivering beside me. "I feel it too," she said, stepping a little further into the house. "He's expecting us. He should have been listening for us. Hello?" she called, louder than I had. "Dr. Brinsley?"

We stood in the cold room, waiting.

"Why isn't he answering us?" whispered Winter.

A huge, empty fireplace to my left had several fire tools hanging from a bar. I picked up the heavy poker. Winter and Boges followed suit, also picking up potential weapons. If Sligo was in here somewhere, we'd need to protect ourselves.

Soundlessly, we crept towards a light at the end of a small hallway behind the staircase, iron tools raised.

Soft music came from behind the door to the room with the light on. Maybe Dr. Brinsley was listening to music and was lost in it. Maybe I was just paranoid. I lowered the poker.

I knocked gently. "It's Cal. I'm here with my friends. We let ourselves in. You asked us to come over at nine, right?"

No answer.

"You two wait here," I whispered. "I'm going in."

I pushed the door open with my shoulder.

The room felt empty, although a fire crackled in a fireplace in the corner. I quickly scanned the scene. Books and papers were scattered around in wild and torn jumbles. The glass doors of a tall bookcase were hanging open, half-off their hinges. A desk in the corner had been violently cleared—pens and paperclips were all over the floor.

Someone had been here. Someone madly searching for something.

I started to fear for Dr. Brinsley.

"This is crazy!" said Boges, who'd come in behind me along with Winter. "Someone has trashed the place!"

Winter gasped. I turned to her—her face was ghostly. Her lips were trembling. She pointed to the ground.

Then I noticed what she was pointing to. Lying half-buried under a series of old, leather-bound volumes.

An out-flung arm.

Brinsley's half-moon spectacles lay on the hearth rug, the golden rims and arms bent out of shape.

I was fixed to the spot. A dark, red stain was spreading over the rug near his body. Even without checking, I knew he was dead.

Winter fell to her knees and started pulling the books and debris off him, turning him over.

"He's dead!" she cried. "Dead! Sligo's been here, and he's done this! He's murdered poor Dr. Brinsley!"

Boges bent down to Winter and pulled her

away from the body. "Don't touch anything," he said. "We've gotta get out of here."

"What about the police?" she asked, getting back to her feet.

"We'll call the cops later—Sligo could still be here," he said. "We'd better run."

I turned around, preparing to walk carefully out of the room the same way I had come in, but as I was about to put my right foot down near Dr. Brinsley's outstretched hand, I paused mid-step. A piece of paper under the desk caught my eye. Familiar words jumped out at me . . . *TOSJORS CELER.*

Cautiously, I bent over and picked it up. The words were part of an old pencil sketch of a ruin, smeared and yellowing with age. The sketch showed crumbling stone walls, collapsed fire-places, vines growing in through unglazed windows, and piles of fallen masonry. This was what he'd wanted to show us.

"Dude, we've gotta get out and call the Garda," Boges said. "Come on, try not to touch anything."

I grabbed Boges's beanie off his head and wrapped my hand in it, turning the door handle and rubbing my prints off it. A sudden gust of wind rushed through from the hall, causing several of the books on the floor to flutter their pages.

From one of them lifted some sort of pamphlet,

rising and diving like a paper plane, almost landing at my feet as if it was trying its best to get my attention.

It was a catalog of books to be sold at an upcoming second-hand book sale. I squinted at the long list of titles printed on it, and there, between John Ferdinand Bottomley's *Roman Epigrams in Irish Poetry* and Alferic Buxtehude's *Romance and Reality: The Celtic Twilight*, I read "Sir James Butler's *Lives of the Saints.*"

"Check this out," I said, picking it up. "Look, the book Dr. Brinsley was talking about. He knew it was going to be in this sale."

"Whatever, Cal," said Boges, practically dragging me out. "Tell us about it when we're not in a room with a dead guy."

I pocketed the catalog, and we hurried out of Brinsley's house, shaken up and shocked.

We half-walked, half-ran from Parnell Square, heading south down the street, stopping only at a pay phone in the foyer of a noisy restaurant.

"Here," said Winter, snatching the phone from me, "I'll do it. Away with ye," she continued, in a thick Irish accent, before speaking into the receiver. "A man has been murdered in Parnell Square," she said, disguising her own accent perfectly. She gave the address to the constable who'd answered, then hung up.

We headed off again, hurrying back to a cafe close to our hotel. We huddled in an empty corner as we all tried to gather our shocked wits. Winter was trembling, and it wasn't just the cold. Boges was shaking too.

"That poor man," murmured Winter. "We were only just talking with him. I can't believe it. He was innocent. Just caught up in this mess for no good reason."

She was right. I felt nauseous. I'd been responsible for another innocent person's death.

"Take a look at this," I said, pulling out the sketch, trying to focus our attention on something else.

"Man," exclaimed Boges. "This has been taken from a crime scene. Could make you an accessory after the fact. I can see the headlines now: 'Psycho Kid strikes in Ireland.'"

Winter glared at the drawing with glassy eyes.

"Look," I pointed. "The motto inscribed in the Jewel is here in this picture."

Although the drawing was faded, and the interior that it depicted was crumbled and decaying, the words that had mesmerized me, drawn my eyes to the sketch—*AMOR ET SUEVRE TOSJORS CELER*—could just be seen in the stucco. They were barely legible in places, letters missing or eroded away, but still enough of them were left for us to be able to recognize the words of the motto inscribed inside the Jewel.

"So it is," said Winter, sounding a little less spooked than a moment ago.

"That's why Dr. Brinsley got so excited when he saw the photo of the Jewel and that enlargement of the inscription," I said. "He recognized the motto from the sketch. He made a connection between the Jewel and this building—whatever it is, wherever it is. We don't know where this sketch fits in," I said, "but whoever killed Dr. Brinsley and trashed the place missed this."

"It must have been Sligo," said Winter. "He must have been after that book—the one Dr. Brinsley told us about. *Lives of the Saints*."

"Probably," I agreed, pulling out the catalog of books. "As I was saying before, it looks like it's going to be here at this sale," I said, pointing at the listing. "It's on in a couple of days, in Kilkenny. At the Black Abbey. We'll have to go there and buy it before someone else does. The Clonmel Way Guest House will just have to wait."

"Dude, it's some kind of antique. It'll cost heaps."

"Might have to steal it," suggested Winter.

"Maybe we won't have to do either of those things," I said. "If the last two lines of the Riddle are in there, like Brinsley said, then we just need to take them out. We can leave the book behind."

"I don't get it," said Winter slowly. "If the last two lines of the Ormond Riddle have just been tucked into this book, wouldn't someone have found them already?"

"I hope not," I said. "It's the only lead we have."

28 DECEMBER

4 days to go . . .

8:00 am

During the darkness of a winter dawn, we all got up and left the hotel behind. We had to move on. Time was ticking down, and we were keen to leave Sligo and the bad memories of our encounters with Brinsley behind. At the bus station we bought tickets to Kilkenny.

We were stinging for Sharkey to return from his reunion so he could join us, but he was going to have to follow us to Kilkenny later.

The Waterford Bed and Breakfast Kilkenny

11:18 am

"We'd love to see the Black Abbey," Winter said to the landlady, Mrs. O'Leary, as we were checking in. "We've heard there's a big book sale happening there shortly."

"Yes, yes, they have it every year," Mrs.

O'Leary cheerfully confirmed. "Fond of books, are you? Well, you might find something very old and very rare for a good price."

She gave us directions to Kilkenny Castle too, and we bundled up and headed for the old attraction.

Kilkenny Castle

2:01 pm

As we walked the paths under the dripping trees, we tried to imagine how the castle would look in the summer, with the huge oak trees full of leaves and the roses blooming.

But after some aimless wandering, I stopped walking and sat down on a low brick wall.

"What is it?" Winter asked, sitting down beside me.

"I feel like we're wasting time. I don't think there are any answers for us here. How about we go back to the Waterford and get our flashlights—we can go check out the Black Abbey tonight, see if we can find more information about the book sale tomorrow. We don't want anyone getting their hands on *Lives of the Saints* before we do."

"Sounds like a good idea to me," she responded.

"Let's move," said Boges, tugging on his beanie.

Black Abbey

8:14 pm

I couldn't help thinking, as we hurried through the dark, sleety night, up the hill towards the Black Abbey, that this could all add up to a big fat zero. All we had was the word of one man—now dead—who thought the last two lines of the Ormond Riddle were in this mysterious book.

I wondered too, why Sligo had murdered Dr. Theophilus Brinsley. Was it out of frustration when he realized that Brinsley didn't have the missing two lines? Or was it because Dr. Brinsley wouldn't tell him where they were?

But what if he *had* told him where they were? That would mean Sligo could already be in Kilkenny. Instinctively, I looked around us, even though it was almost impossible to see anything in the darkness.

The bulk of the Black Abbey loomed ahead. It was a low building, with a short, square tower, its turrets barely discernible against the night sky. As we approached the stone wall that surrounded it, I grabbed the others, stopping them in their tracks.

"There's somebody there, look. See that van parked over there?"

"Dude, let's check out who it is. I've been

wondering whether Sligo would be here already," said Boges.

"Me too," I admitted.

"Me three," added Winter, gripping my arm tightly.

We pressed on cautiously, trying to keep out of sight of anyone near the van.

The van had its headlights on, illuminating the door to a stone building adjacent to the Black Abbey that I had mistakenly thought was part of the abbey itself.

"What are they doing?" whispered Winter.

"Looks like they're unloading something," said Boges, close behind me. We watched two people vanish through the doorway.

"They're unloading books," I said. "Setting up for tomorrow."

I put my hand in my pocket and grabbed my flashlight. This was a piece of unexpected good luck. Maybe we could sneak in and get a preview.

The three of us hurried through the drizzle and over to the deserted van. Inside, it was empty. They must have only just unloaded the last of the boxes.

Silently, we sneaked inside the building, following the same path the people from the van had taken. The sound of footsteps and voices echoed from the other end of the corridor.

"Quick! They're coming back!" I hissed.

I opened the nearest door, and the three of us scrambled inside, closing the door again behind us. I pressed my ear up against it, listening for movement. I heard the movers pass by outside in the corridor, then they left, slamming the door behind them.

A few moments later, the van started up and drove away.

"OK," I breathed, slowly turning the handle of the door and checking the corridor outside. "We're alone now. Let's see what we can find."

The lights had been switched off, but we used our flashlights to guide us. We hurried to the end of the dark corridor where a door on my left and a flight of stairs on my right formed a T-junction. Passing my flashlight to Boges, I tried the door. It wasn't locked. I opened it and walked inside.

Ahead of us were three long, trestle tables, each one covered with tablecloths and piled high with books for tomorrow's sale.

My heart was like a drum, pounding as excitement mounted in me. Winter and Boges rushed to the books and started looking through them, and I quickly followed. Somewhere in this collection, I hoped, was the book containing the missing last two lines of the Riddle. The answer to the mystery of the Ormond Singularity was at our fingertips.

"OK, dude," said Boges, "I'll take this table, Winter's on that one," he said, pointing to the furthest one. "You take the middle."

The smell of musty, old books in the freezing air filled my nose as I ran the flashlight over the spines and covers of the ancient books. Some were in Latin with old-fashioned marbled endpapers. Some were in Gaelic with faded gold lettering on their covers.

After about half an hour, I'd been through every book on my table.

"I think I'm done, guys. Either of you have any luck?"

"No," they both answered, their disappointment obvious in their tones.

It wasn't here. What were we going to do now? What if Sligo already had it?

"Quick, hide!" I ordered the others, as voices interrupted the air.

We scrambled under the trestle table furthest from the door, huddling in the darkness, shielded, I hoped, by the tablecloth and other book-covered trestle tables. Someone was in the building with us.

Footsteps approached. The door handle squeaked as it was opened, and someone came into the cluttered space. I didn't dare move to see who it was.

Foreign flashlight beams started darting around the room, wavering across the floor and over the tables. We squashed ourselves as hard as we could against the wall, hoping the light wouldn't pick us up. I bumped my body into a box that had been shoved under the table.

I peered into the box and focused on a thin book sitting on top. The lettering was barely visible in the dark, but the shape of the title had grabbed me.

My eyes widened with stunned surprise. My head started spinning, not because of the imminent threat of being discovered, but because I was staring straight at the book we were after! I couldn't believe it! I bit my tongue and tried to keep still.

Once satisfied that everything was in order, the security guard, or whoever it was, stepped back out into the corridor, closing the door behind them.

I exhaled and grabbed the book out of the box. I turned to my friends and shone my flashlight on it so they could both see what I had found.

"You found it!" said Boges, trying not to shout.

"Amazing!" Winter smiled, shuffling in closer and wiping dust from its cover. "No point sticking around any longer. Hold onto it for dear life and follow me out of here!"

Winter crawled out from under the table, then stealthily led us over to the door, down the corridor, outside and away from the Black Abbey.

We ran, without stopping, all the way back to the Waterford.

The Waterford Bed and Breakfast Kilkenny

10:01 pm

Breathlessly, I opened Butler's *Lives of the Saints* as Winter and Boges practically bounced with excitement on the bed beside me. My hands were shaking as I flicked through the heavy paper with its dense printing, checking page after page.

Pretty quickly my excitement vanished.

"There's nothing in it. Nothing!" I yelled, throwing the book down on the floor. "Just page after page of garbage about ancient, old saints!"

"Don't give up so quickly," said Winter, hopping off the bed and picking the book back up. "Maybe the lines have been written *in* somewhere—along an inside margin or something. Let me have a careful look."

She plopped down on the bed again and

slowly, methodically, started turning every page, running her finger down the central margins of each one before turning to the next page. She used her flashlight to throw extra light on the yellowing pages.

"I just don't know how we're going to beat the deadline," I said. "I was so sure we were on the right track, but we still don't really even know what we're doing, where we should be going. We don't even know what we're looking for."

Winter turned her smoky eyes on me. "Cal," she said, "I have a feeling that everything's going to fall into place for us. Everything will come together. You'll see."

Outside, the wind had picked up, and heavy rain was driving against the window, rattling the wooden frames. I went over to pull the heavy curtains shut, but before I did, I peered out into the darkness. I had a horrible feeling that someone was out there. I dragged the curtains across and sat back down.

"No good," admitted Winter, shutting the book after her closer examination.

"Still thinking everything's going to work out?" I asked her.

She replied with an unimpressed look.

"My turn," said Boges, before he too went through it. He ran a magnifying glass carefully over every page and margin and peered down the cracking spine of the old-fashioned book.

But there was nothing in there that we wanted.

We sat in a triangle, staring blankly at each other. None of us had any energy or will left to bother saying anything. Eventually we just picked ourselves up and called it a night, crawling into bed, hoping tomorrow would deliver us a miracle.

29 DECEMBER

3 days to go . . .

10:16 am

"I just have a couple more family meals to survive here," Sharkey joked, over the phone, "before I can come to you guys. I've had enough of the Sharkey family, to be honest. They just want to talk, talk, talk. The murder of Dr. Brinsley has been massive news," he said. "Everyone knows about it. At this stage the Garda don't have any leads."

"At least *I'm* not on their radar," I said. That was one good thing. We'd avoided talking about it, but the death of Dr. Brinsley was hanging over us like a black cloud, reminding us of the huge danger that accompanied our quest.

"So you've checked the book thoroughly?" he asked. "Been over the margins?"

"Nelson, we've gone over it with a fine-tooth comb. If the last two lines of the Ormond Riddle were ever in that book, they sure aren't now."

Sharkey groaned. "What a waste of time," he

said. "Look, I have to go again, but you three be very careful," he warned. "I'll join you as soon as I can. Don't go anywhere you don't need to go, OK?"

"We're leaving Kilkenny and going to Carrick-on-Suir today," I said. "Off to the Clonmel Way Guest House, where my dad stayed last year."

"Good idea. Stay safe, and I'll see you soon."

2:21 pm

A bus took us all the way down to Carrick-on-Suir. We stepped out into another cold, gray day, and as I walked down the cobbled streets with my two friends, I felt a confused mix of emotions: sad that this was where my dad first became so sick, but almost excited to be walking where he'd walked.

The drawings that I still carried with me had started me off on this huge journey. Time was running out. I only had three days left. It wasn't just about survival anymore.

"Oh, look!" cried Winter, pointing to a decaying tower sticking up over some long gray walls in the distance. "Do you think that's one of Black Tom's castles?"

I checked the map I'd picked up at the bus station. "It sure is," I said. "Ormond Castle. We should check that out, but first we've got to find the guesthouse. It should be just up here," I said, indicating the end of a narrowing road lined with houses.

Clonmel Way Guest House was the last building in a row of homes that backed onto the broad quay along the river. I could see the sign, cut in the shape of a salmon, swinging in the wind.

Clonmel Way Guest House
Carrick-on-Suir

3:20 pm

The narrow, two-story property was painted blue and white and had a small winter garden.

I went to open the gate and stopped abruptly. Winter gasped behind me. Boges muttered under his breath.

There in the rusty wrought iron of the gate, in an enamel oval, was the *number five*, just like in my dad's drawing!

"See?" cried Winter. "I told you things were going to come together!"

The drawing suddenly became clear—Dad had been trying to point out this place! I felt a surge of new energy powering through me, easing my disappointment about not finding the last two lines of the Riddle. We'd just have to find another way to get to the right destination.

I opened the gate and ran up the short path, knocking on the bright red door. A brass plaque above the doorway read: Clonmel Way Guest House – Imelda Fitzgerald, Proprietor.

A fair woman with rosy cheeks opened the door. She smiled broadly and welcomed us inside.

"I have plenty of rooms this time of year," she said. "You look like you could do with some good Irish scones and a cup of tea. Come in out of the cold."

We happily followed her into the cozy interior—a small foyer where plump crimson couches and armchairs were grouped around a blazing fire. Old sepia photos above the fireplace showed horses towing barges along the riverside.

I introduced myself as Matt Marlow, along with my friends Grace and Josh.

"Like I say," said Mrs. Fitzgerald, "it's not the best time of year. Doesn't do the place justice. Still, there's plenty to do, even in winter, and we have a couple of cots down on the river for the use of our guests."

"Cots?" asked Boges, a funny look on his face.

Mrs. Fitzgerald laughed. "That's the name of the famous Carrick fishing boats. The Carrick cots. That's if you like messing around in boats."

Mrs. Fitzgerald chatted on. She knew all about Black Tom's Ormond Castle, built at the end of the town. It was a feature of the township and a reason why visitors came to Carrick.

"It's the best example of an Elizabethan manor house in the land," she gloated. "I heard that the ruins of one of Black Tom's other old castles is being shipped back to the USA, brick by brick, to be rebuilt in Kentucky. Those Americans," she said, with a smile. "Do you know they have London Bridge in Arizona?"

Mrs. Fitzgerald drew the curtains aside, and we looked out the window to the rear of the property. There was a short yard, surrounded by a low fence, and beyond that was a broad pathway along the river, wide enough for horses.

The tide was out, and a few small canoes lay half on their sides in the muddy sand, awaiting the surge that would lift them up and float them again. In a field across the river, a couple of horses leaned over a fence, just visible in the cold, misty air.

Mrs. Fitzgerald noticed the direction of my gaze. "You like horses?" she asked. "They belong to the travelers—the gypsies. You could probably rent a couple if you like riding."

"I'd love to, but I'm not actually here for a

holiday," I said, turning back from the window. I wanted information, so I needed to tell her who I was. Kind of.

"My *uncle*," I lied, "Tom Ormond, stayed here last year. Until he became sick."

Mrs. Fitzgerald's face lost its smile. "God rest his soul. You're Tom Ormond's nephew?"

"I am," I said, hoping she wasn't going to think too much about it and ask me any difficult questions. "These are my friends, *Grace* and *Josh*," I repeated nervously.

"I was so sorry to hear about his illness . . . and then his death," she said solemnly. "It was a terrible job I had, packing up his clothing and things. He was such a lovely fellow. You've come to see where he stayed before he was sick?"

"I'd like to see his room," I said, nodding. "We were very close. I miss him very much."

"Of course you do," she said, picking up a key from the hall table. "Nothing's changed in here. It's exactly as it was when he was staying. We haven't had many guests this year," she admitted, with a hint of embarrassment. "Come with me."

We followed her down the hallway to where she opened a door at the end and stepped back, allowing us to walk inside ahead of her. It was a small room, painted white, and in an alcove on the right was a bay window with a vase of yellow paper roses. A sink, a hot plate and an electric kettle formed the kitchen area.

"Your uncle cooked on that," Mrs. Fitzgerald said, noticing me looking at the hot plate.

"Uncle Tom? Cooking?" I asked, surprised. "That's weird. My *aunt* never let him cook at home—he was horrible! Aunt Win used to—" I stopped speaking as memories of my home life with Mum and Dad surfaced. I felt Winter's light touch on the back of my hand. "He was always burning things. Even at family barbecues. I guess being here alone forced him to give it another try."

"I'm sorry to tell you he hadn't improved," confessed Mrs. Fitzgerald, with a chuckle. "One night I caught him trying to cook this sloppy soup." She wrinkled up her nose in distaste. "Some sort of vegetable and herb soup. He must have let it boil for so long that it all just turned to mush."

I smiled, picturing Dad trying his best.

"I came in to drop off some clean laundry," continued Mrs. Fitzgerald, "and I could see past his shoulder and into the kitchen sink. He'd made such a mess! There was a pile of veggie skins, herbs and even something that looked like ferns on the counter." She shook her head. "He hadn't told me he'd be in for dinner that night, but really, I could have arranged something else for him.

Parsley, coriander and basil I understand, but ferns? I think I might have offended him with my offer of a slice of shepherd's pie to have instead."

I wandered further into the room. Beyond the kitchen, a bed, a table and chair, a fireplace set with pinecones and a big, carved wardrobe completed the furnishings.

A wardrobe!

A *carved* wardrobe!

I stopped, rooted to the spot. Boges and Winter crashed into me.

"Move along there, dude," said Boges. Until he saw the reason for my shock. "A wardrobe!"

"A wardrobe!" Winter cried, bouncing up and down. "I told you! I told you! We're on the right track. The carved doors!"

"Er, yes," said Mrs. Fitzgerald, clearly confused about our excitement over a basic piece of furniture. She must have thought we'd never seen a wardrobe before! "'Tis rather grand, I suppose," she continued. "Big and roomy."

The telephone rang from down the hall, and she excused herself before hurriedly shuffling away.

The fancy carving and the big metal ring at the front of the wardrobe were distinct—this was definitely the door from my dad's drawing! I darted across the room and opened it. It creaked as I peered inside.

It had an odd, woody smell, a tall space for hanging clothes, and an open shelf on the right on top of three drawers. Quickly, I opened them all, one after the other, but they were empty.

I squatted down to check the dark space underneath the drawers.

"There's nothing in here," I said, straightening up, disappointment rearing its ugly head again. I felt my fists clench. "We've come all this way—for what? We haven't found the last lines of the Riddle, and now there's nothing in this stupid thing!"

"Cal," said Winter, "don't panic. All your dad's drawings mean something. We've been able to figure them out. We can do it with this one too."

"But maybe what he wanted us to see isn't here anymore," I said. "Which means the drawing was pointless. A dead end."

"Let's just all take a breath and wait a moment," continued Winter, staring inside the wardrobe. "Something could suddenly make sense."

I turned my head, about to whack the side in hopelessness, when Winter shoved herself in between me and the door.

"What's this?" she said, running a finger over the paper lining on the inside of the door. "This isn't lining, it's a map!"

She moved over so I could have a closer look.

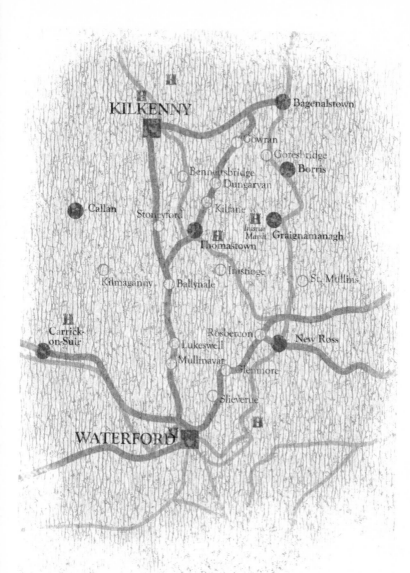

I looked closer. Right at eye level, and right where I was staring, was a place name—Graignamanagh, and just up from it was another place name—Kilfane.

G'managh and Kilfane! The place names on the tracing paper!

I swung around to the others, pulling off my backpack. "The tracing paper! That's why Dad drew this wardrobe!"

"It *is* a map!" shouted Boges, peering closer at the lining. "I see what you mean! C'mon, dude! Hurry up and find the tracing paper!"

I rummaged through my backpack and carefully lifted it out.

My fingers were trembling with excitement as I held the tracing paper up against the map, lining it up against the inside of the wardrobe door until the two names written by Dad—G'managh and Kilfane—were perfectly superimposed over the names on the old map.

Between them was the black dot.

"Wow!" breathed Winter.

"Will you look at that!" Boges spluttered.

I stood back, holding the tracing paper to see that now the black dot sat right on top of another name.

"Inisrue Marsh!" cried Winter. "Your dad was

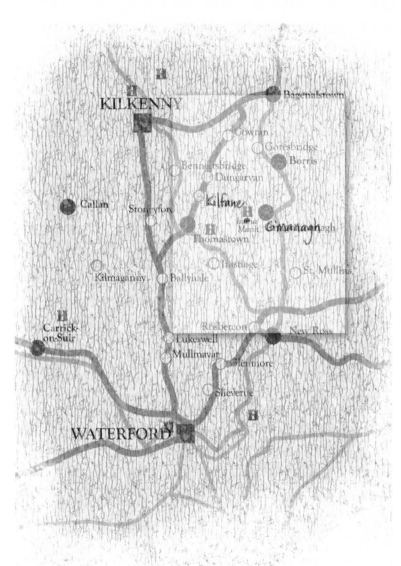

telling us that we have to go to Inisrue Marsh! This is incredible! Now we know where to go!"

"I wonder what's there?" said Boges. He traced a finger along from our present location on the riverside at the edge of the village of Carrick-on-Suir, moving up to the black dot. "Across the river and north," he said, pointing. "It's not that far away."

The sound of scuffling and thudding, topped by a woman's scream, shocked us away from the map.

"Mrs. Fitzgerald? You OK?" called Boges, racing to the door and sticking his head around it.

Footsteps pounded down the hallway, and Boges jumped back, slammed the door shut and turned the key. I'd never seen him move so fast.

"Sligo!" he hissed, horrified. "And Zombie Two! How did they find us?"

"Sligo?" Winter repeated nervously. "He's *really* here! I guess that means he's definitely canceled his New Year's Eve Ball!"

I grabbed the tracing paper, shoved it in my backpack next to *Lives of the Saints*, whipped it over my arm and hurled myself across the room, knocking the yellow roses to the floor in the process. I wrenched the window open and gestured to Boges and Winter to climb through.

As soon as they'd landed on the other side, I heaved myself halfway over the sill, ready to leap into the dark drizzle of the oncoming night. From somewhere outside I could hear Mrs. Fitzgerald calling for help and neighbors responding with alarmed shouts.

"Call the Garda!" I heard someone scream.

Sligo and Zombie Two were battering on our room's door.

"Jump!" shouted Boges, from below.

I pushed off and thudded down. I scrambled to my feet and followed my friends over the back fence, heading for the quay.

"They've escaped out the window!" Sligo's voice boomed from behind us. "Get the car!"

"Run for your life!" Boges shouted to me. "Don't follow us—we'll do what we can to steer them away from you!"

"But—"

"Just go!" he ordered, slowing to wave his arms and grab Sligo's attention.

"Boges!" I shouted, worried about my friends. "Winter, you have to run!"

"Go!" she shouted.

4:46 pm

I shot away over the back fence, down the quayside and then towards the low stone bridge that crossed the river.

Freezing rain started pouring down in sheets, drenching me as I bolted over the bridge. It was almost impossible to see where I was going—everything ahead of me was a wet, gray blur.

Suddenly something glowed in that gray blur. Headlights! A car skidded and swerved towards me, flying recklessly along the quayside.

I ran out of its wild path, but it jerked and twisted after me, tires squealing on the slippery ground. It spun and screeched to a halt.

Seconds later, Zombie Two had kicked the front car door wide open and was barreling after me on foot, pounding down the cobblestones, eyes locked onto me.

I was sure I could get away because he was so big and lumbering, and I was faster, but my sneakers skidded on a slippery stone, and I went flying, crash-landing on my stomach.

I scrambled to my feet and looked back, but I couldn't see him.

The car started again—he must have run back to it! I was frantic; I couldn't let Sligo get his hands on me, let alone the tracing paper and everything else in my backpack.

I ran alongside the river as it curved around a bend. Pulled up on the stones was one of the canoe-style boats that Mrs. Fitzgerald had called a Carrick cot, almost completely covered by a canvas tarp. Quick as a flash, I wrenched my backpack off and flung it perfectly into the opening in the skiff, and then I took off in the opposite direction.

I could hear the car coming behind me, accelerating, and I knew I had to find a thin alley where a car couldn't follow. A narrow bridge crossed the river a little distance away, and I pelted across it.

I'd hoped the narrowness would stop Sligo's car, but all it did was slow it down. They forged ahead with only inches on either side between their vehicle and the bridge's brick walls.

There were fewer houses on this side of the river, and between two of them was a grassy field which led to a dense forested area—my chance of escape. I ran for it.

In seconds, I was sinking up to my ankles in boggy marshland. I struggled and staggered unevenly, slowing down to a snail's pace. I wrenched my legs out of the bog and plowed ahead, desperately aiming for firmer ground.

When I finally felt solid ground under my feet, I kicked mud off my legs and ran again, straight for the forest.

A blow on my left sent me flying to the ground, sideways.

Zombie Two had tackled me. He must have seen that I was heading for the forest and figured out a way to grab me from the other side. I struggled and kicked, but he had me in a painful wristlock, twisting my arm behind me.

He yelled and spat at me as he dragged me by my feet over to his car. I clawed at the muddy ground, trying uselessly to break free.

Once we reached the car, Zombie Two picked me up and tossed me inside, then climbed in and practically sat on top of me to keep me restrained.

A shadowy figure in the front seat turned around.

Sligo was sitting at the wheel.

"We meet again," he growled, his cravat crooked and crumpled around his thick neck. "I'll make this simple for you. If you want to live, you'd better start talking. You tell me about the Ormond Singularity, in exchange for your life."

I gulped, trying to get my breath back and clear my head.

"Speak!" he demanded. "What do you have for me, boy? Do you want to live? Where are the Ormond Riddle and the Ormond Jewel?"

"Back home where you'll never find them!" I yelled, wriggling under Zombie Two's stifling mass.

"*Home*? A delinquent like you doesn't have a home," he sniggered, sending shivers down my spine. "Neither does that little viper, Winter. Don't you worry, I'll find the Jewel and the Riddle. I'll track down your buddies too, including my *precious* ward—I know she's here with you, and I've read the notes she wrote."

"Then you know as much as I do!"

"Did your father find something here?" Sligo snapped. "Tell me what you are doing in Carrick!"

"They say travel broadens the mind," I wheezed.

Zombie Two pushed his weight down on me even more, clearly not finding my joke very funny. I groaned in pain.

"You obviously don't value your life, Callum Ormond," said Sligo, viciously reversing the car, then accelerating forward. "Winter didn't give me any trouble until she met up with *you*. This is personal now. This *ends* now," he said, with severe finality.

The car sped along, driving through the mist and rain.

"We're about to go to a little-known local attraction. Have you ever heard of the Dundrum Oubliette?"

I hadn't heard of it, but whatever it was, I

knew it meant trouble.

"I said, have you heard of the Dundrum Oubliette?" he repeated.

"Yes. You just mentioned it a second ago."

"Think you're funny, eh?" hissed Sligo. "I'll be the one having the last laugh."

My blood turned ice-cold as I considered the fact that this was also the man who had left me to die in an oil tank. This was also the man who had left *Winter*—the girl who was supposed to be in his care—to die.

5:23 pm

We drove for another twenty minutes or so, passing the dark Irish countryside. I tried to sit up a bit better to see where we were going, but it wasn't easy—Zombie Two kept pushing me face down into the backseat.

I caught a glimpse of a Y-intersection and could just make out a row of big stones and a signpost pointing to the road on the right that read something like "Roland's Tower." Sligo wrenched the steering wheel to the left, and the car rattled and jerked its way down a dirt road instead.

Eventually he pulled up at a gate. Zombie Two eased off me, and I sat up a bit. "Dundrum Oubliette," I read to myself. "Open June—October."

Sligo climbed out of the car, stepping into

the pouring rain. He dragged a pair of heavy-duty bolt cutters out of the trunk, stalked over to the gate and cut right through the chains woven through them. I peered ahead, trying to see through the rain drumming on the windshield. Some distance ahead, I could make out what looked like a half-fallen wall.

Sligo lumbered back into the driver's seat and drove the car through the gateway and up to the stony structure.

"Get him out," he ordered Zombie Two, muttering about the rain as he lifted his heavy body out of the driver's seat again. "Destroy his phone!"

Zombie Two hauled me out into the cold night air and patted me down. My phone was in my backpack that I'd chucked into one of the Carrick cots, so I didn't have anything on me for them to destroy.

"No phone," he yelled out.

Sligo shone a flashlight ahead of him while Zombie Two dragged me along after his boss, my arms twisted up behind my back. I was led down some stone steps and into what must have been a courtyard hundreds of years ago, but was now more like a flat, crumbling rock. I noticed Sligo was also carrying a grappling hook on a chain.

What was an oubliette? I wondered, panic rising.

Maybe it was good that I didn't know what I was in for . . .

In the middle of the courtyard was a round drain, covered by a heavy iron grille. Sligo knelt beside it. He put down his flashlight and wedged one of the barbs of the grappling hook under one of the bars on the grille.

His flashlight sat in a puddle, directing light onto a plaque that had been attached to the ground near the drain.

"Hold on to the little scumbag while I get the cover off," Sligo yelled to Zombie Two.

Zombie gripped me while Sligo went back to the car. With the other end of the chain attached to the front of the vehicle, Sligo jumped in behind the wheel and revved it up. He slammed the accelerator, and the car reversed, ripping the cover off the drain opening. It rolled and landed a few yards away.

I struggled against Zombie Two as horrifying images of the inside of the oil tank came back to me. Was Sligo going to shove me in a drain? Drown me in storm water?

Sligo returned and scowled at me, an evil leer on his pudgy face. "As you can see from the sign, this is an oubliette," his voice boomed, over the easing rain. "I trust you can read, but maybe if you'd listened better in school, you'd know that the French word 'oubliette' means 'place to forget.' You might also have learned that an oubliette is a medieval prison, made for those who had displeased the local noblemen. The offender was dropped into the hole and, well, *forgotten!* They were abandoned in these deep underground dungeons, sometimes knee deep in water, sewage, rats . . . but this one has an extra attraction of another kind." Sligo paused and grinned. He turned to Zombie Two. "Drag him over so he can see."

Zombie Two followed orders and pushed me towards the hole. It gaped like nothing but a black circle until Sligo shone his flashlight down.

I croaked in horror!

I was staring down into a seemingly bottomless pit, with a *huge* spike spearing up from the darkness. Its wicked point glinted in the flashlight beam.

"You should thank me for it, really," mocked Sligo. "Being impaled on that spike, as excruciatingly unpleasant as I believe it will be, means a much quicker death than starvation. The treacherous bogs have already proven to be a great place for dumping a troublesome body, but this is far more gruesome, don't you think?" he said, to Zombie Two.

Zombie Two bellowed with laughter.

"Although it was fun," Sligo continued, "watching Rathbone struggle in the mud."

"You murdered Rathbone?" I screeched.

"Enough!" he screeched back. "Throw him in!"

I shouted and screamed and struggled uselessly in Zombie Two's iron grip. He began lifting me up, and I kicked out as Sligo grabbed my other shoulder and upper arm. Together they were about to hurl me into the black hole! I would be speared like a piece of meat on a spit!

This couldn't be happening—but it was!

I fought with all my strength, but slowly, inevitably, they hoisted me over the edge. I stretched my legs out wide, making it impossible for them to drop me into the narrow passage. Zombie Two saw what I was trying to do, and he kicked my feet back together and into the hole— leaving me with nothing to keep me above the surface.

Then they let go.

Instinctively, as I fell, I swerved like a diver in a sideways twist, trying to curl my body around the spike.

I crashed down painfully, the flesh on my thighs and arms grazing right off as my clothes tore, and I collided with the jagged, stony walls. I landed with a back-breaking thud.

I was hurt, but I'd avoided being impaled on the spike!

Stunned and winded, I looked up at the pale circle of night sky above me. The grille had already been returned to its original position— the straight lines of the bars drew shadows over my battered body.

I was trapped, bleeding and soaking wet, in the bottom of an oubliette, in the dead of winter, somewhere in Ireland.

As if to push my despair just that little bit further, a clap of thunder sounded, and the rain began pouring down again in buckets.

I tried to get to my feet, but slipped in the pool of water. I wanted to scream out, but I stopped myself, thinking it would be better if Sligo and Zombie Two thought I was already dead.

The sound of Sligo's car disappeared into the night, and I was alone. Abandoned. *Forgotten*.

He'd killed Rathbone.

Was I about to die next?

6:29 pm

I slumped against the wall and looked up, the rain relentlessly pelting down on my face.

There had to be a way out of here. Surely I could climb up the wall somehow. Maybe—if I could get up to the top and find a strong enough foothold—I could push the grille off.

The numbness wore off from my shaking limbs, and I was aware of how uncomfortable I was, sitting on the stones, or rocks, or whatever it was that covered the ground of this hole. I struggled to sit up and twisted around to see what I was sitting on.

I jumped up in horror.

What had cushioned my fall were piles of dead

leaves on top of old, broken bones! The bones of other prisoners who had lived and died down here, forgotten centuries ago!

Stay calm, said a voice in my head. *Think, Cal, think.*

I tried to control my breathing and let my eyes adjust even more to the darkness. I shielded my face from the rain and looked around. I could see I was in a circular space, slightly wider than the opening many yards above, with sloping stone walls covered in thick, slippery moss.

Over the bones and the dust, I felt my way around the walls. They were wet and slimy, and worse, they were funnel-shaped, so that the opening at the top part of the oubliette closed over me like the neck of a bottle. Climbing out looked seriously unlikely . . .

I moved my legs to check they were OK, sloshing them around in the water that was building up like a well. Next I checked my arms and remembered the distress beacon Boges had given me! My watch!

I squinted at it on my wrist, but could hardly see anything. I rubbed its face with my fingers and almost choked when I realized it was completely shattered—the glass had been crushed in my fall. The insides of the watch were destroyed and saturated.

The beacon was not going to save me.

With trembling fingers, I pressed the winder of the watch anyway.

Nothing happened. I stared at the watch face. There was no sound. There was no pulsing blue light.

Again and again I pressed on the tiny winder, until the whole watch fell away in pieces, and all that was left on my wrist was the band.

Nobody knew I was here, and the sign on the gate said that this place was closed until June. I was stuffed.

I grabbed at the slippery, moss-covered stone walls again, trying to find any possible hand grips. I made several attempts to climb the wall, but just fell crashing to the ground, drenching myself over and over again.

No matter how hard I tried, it was impossible—I wasn't getting anywhere. My hands were scraped and cut from trying. The small indentations that I managed to hook my fingers onto crumbled away under my weight, weakened by constant water erosion.

After about two hours of useless clawing, I crouched in the damp darkness, exhausted. I made a pile out of the broken bones, to sit on above the rising water level.

It was freezing. I felt as cold as I was when

Three-O locked me in that seafood freezer. I was on the verge of death then, and I was pretty sure I was on the verge of death now.

Sligo's gloating words returned to me as I stared at the spike. Maybe he was right. Maybe it would have been better *not* to have avoided it.

30 DECEMBER

2 days to go . . .

Dundrum Oubliette

11:30 am

I spent hours yelling out, begging someone to come and help me out of this death trap. I shouted until my voice was hoarse.

More hours passed, and I tried to soak up the few weak rays of winter sun that made their way down to the bottom of the oubliette, trying to get my clothes dry after the intense rain of last night. The icy water had risen past my knees, and even though I was doing all I could to stay out of it, I just couldn't get completely clear and dry. I was worried about what another sub-zero night down here would do to me—I didn't think I could take it.

I shuddered as a faint beam of light shone on the bones of the others who'd perished here before me. I wondered if they had remained hopeful until the very end. Or if they had just given up. I was in Ireland and so close to solving the Ormond Singularity, but every second I felt more and more convinced that this was it for me. I was going to die a horrible, slow, lonely death.

3:17 pm

Could I make a rope out of my clothes? I wondered. If so, maybe I could wrap it around the spike and shinny up, closer to the grille. Maybe, once there, I could loop the rope around one of the bars and somehow haul myself up, kick the bars and swing out . . .

I had to give it a try. My hands were shivering as I slipped out of my T-shirt and undershirt, pulled my tattered sweater and coat back on, and started ripping the material into strips.

When I guessed I had enough length of knotted fabric, I wrapped it around the spike and made a start on shinnying up. I grabbed the rope tightly in my hands, clamping my muddy, wet sneakers around the spike, like some crazy climbing frog. My hands and feet slipped painfully down again, and I smacked my chin on the spike. My skin scraped off from the sharp flakes of rust under the slime, and I fell back, wincing in pain.

Over and over, I threw myself up the spike, trying to grab it and haul myself up. But over and over I found myself painfully slipping down again, until the palms of my hands were skinned raw, and the fabric on the inside thighs of my jeans was torn and ragged.

It was no use. No way was I going to be able to get up this deadly, giant needle.

I was freezing, bleeding, hungry and exhausted. I collapsed on top of the pile of bones and started trying to send telepathic thoughts out to Winter and Boges. I hoped they were OK and somewhere safe. It was like I was back at the cemetery, when they were searching for me, not knowing where to dig. I knew they'd be going out of their minds with worry.

Even if they sensed I was still alive somewhere, the odds of them finding me were about a million to one.

10:37 pm

Another night in the oubliette. I was faint and dizzy. My body was jolting with shock from the cold, and my teeth chattered constantly, desperately trying to shake me into some semblance of warmth. My hands were swollen and painful, and I was having trouble thinking straight.

I thought of how this journey had begun with a drawing of an angel. The Ormond Angel was supposed to come to the aid of the heir in his time of need.

"I need you now!" I screeched into the air, willing him to swoop down and save me. "Where are you?!"

All I could hear was water dripping.

"I'm the heir! Come and save me!"

Again, all I could hear was dripping.

"There is no Ormond Angel," I muttered to myself.

Right at that moment I thought I saw something move in a fresh circle of light above me. I shook my head, convinced hallucinations were starting.

But then something moved again. The shadows over me definitely shifted.

I stared up. It seemed like a figure was standing on top of the grille.

Then the figure bent down and peered into the hole. White light shone around the figure's head like a halo, and what looked like a huge, folded wing peeked over its shoulder.

I blinked. *Was* I hallucinating? Had the stress and fear made me crazy?

The figure shimmered above me.

Was it the Angel? Just in time?

"H-h-hello?" I murmured.

I blinked as a flashlight beam suddenly fell on my face.

"Cal?"

A voice! A voice I knew!

"Cal? You OK?"

Relief flooded my body.

"Rafe," I wailed, like a baby. "Uncle Rafe!"

It wasn't the Ormond Angel above me, but my uncle Rafe. What I'd thought was a rounded wing was now revealed as a huge coil of rope, backlit by powerful lights—probably his car headlights.

"Hang on, boy, I'm going to get you out of there," he said, moving the grille away with a crow bar. He lowered a rope with a loop at the end, which I quickly fixed around my waist.

"I'm r-r-ready!" I called out, and immediately he used all his strength to haul me out of the dreaded oubliette.

Once he could reach me, Rafe grabbed onto my arms and pulled me all the way out and onto the ground. I lay there, numb and shivering, unable to move. He wrapped a blanket around me, picked me up and carried me to the car. He sat me upright in the passenger seat, slammed the door, then ran around to the driver's side, turning the ignition and cranking the heat full blast.

"Look at you," he said, leaning over and rubbing my hands. He passed me a bottle of water. "Lucky I found you when I did. Any serious injuries?"

I shook my head and sipped from the bottle. "Just c-c-cold," I stuttered. "H-h-how on earth,"

I said, barely able to control my words through my freezing lips, "did you find me?"

He took a deep breath, seeming unsure where to start.

"It's a long story," he began, turning all the air vents on the rental car in my direction. "As soon as we were notified that you'd been arrested after ramming the police station back home, your mum and I rushed in to see you. But," he said, driving us away from the oubliette, "it wasn't you we found there, was it?"

I shook my head gently, picturing Ryan Spencer, and smiled with dry, cracked lips.

"I'd heard that the authorities believed you were a flight risk, so as soon as I realized an 'impostor' had been arrested, and that the whole thing had been a setup, I knew you'd flown the coop."

"So you saw Ryan?" I asked, finally starting to recover my speech.

"We sure did," he said, with a wide grin and a sparkle in his eyes. "I never thought I'd see the day, Cal. I never thought we'd see Samuel again."

"And Mum?"

"Your mum was extremely overwhelmed," he said firmly.

"In a good way, right?"

"Certainly, Cal," he said hesitantly. "This year has been one long, emotional roller coaster. The highs *and* lows just keep on coming."

"What's wrong?" I asked, sensing he was holding something back. I knew I should be slowly warming up, but my body was still shivering, and I was finding it hard to understand what Rafe was saying.

"Your mother and I had a very serious argument," he admitted. "I discovered that she'd been secretly dealing with the family lawyer, working on finding the Ormond Singularity."

I coughed, almost choked. "What? Mum? Working with Rathbone?"

Rafe looked surprised that I knew who he was talking about.

"Look, I don't know how involved she is," he said, "so don't go jumping to any conclusions, OK? But after she told me Rathbone had left for Ireland, and then your missing twin was arrested, I started piecing things together. As soon as I realized Boges had gone on some mysterious 'school trip' I figured you'd both come here together. When I heard that Vulkan Sligo was on his way here too, I knew you were in terrible danger—more than ever before."

"You were right," I said. "I survived Sligo, but Rathbone wasn't as lucky. He's dead."

Rafe looked shocked.

"Sligo murdered him," I explained. "Tossed

him in a bog."

Rafe just shook his head. "I knew Sligo would be tracking you," he continued, as he drove, "so I tracked *him* to Clonmel Way Guest House, where I discovered what had happened. Your friends Winter and Boges filled me in on what had gone down."

"So they're OK?" I asked, relief hitting the deep-frozen organ that was my heart.

"They're both fine. They chased after you for a while, but lost Sligo's car. Winter had even borrowed a horse in an effort to keep up, but she simply couldn't."

"Borrowed a horse?"

"She found one in a field belonging to the travelers and jumped the nearest fence to chase after you."

I pulled the blanket around me, starting to thaw out, trying to imagine Winter "borrowing" a horse like that.

"They haven't been able to go back to the guesthouse. They're actually huddling down with some gypsies."

"The gypsies Winter borrowed the horse from?"

"Yes, they're camped out in some tents and trailers by the river, a few miles south of the guesthouse. We're heading there now."

"So how did you know I was down in that

pit?" I asked again, my teeth finally easing in their chattering.

"I didn't. Not at first. But I started following the tracks on the road—the rain had washed the top layer off—but the road Sligo had taken only forked off to two places."

I remembered the Y-intersection I'd spotted as I struggled with Zombie Two in the back of the car.

"I wound up at Roland's Tower first, searching for you there. Once I'd exhausted that possibility, I backtracked and headed towards the oubliette. I was standing there, thinking it was a dead end, when I heard a cry and realized I was standing on top of you. The rest is history."

I let my head fall back into the car seat, still struggling to believe I'd been saved. By my uncle.

11:52 pm

As we turned back into Carrick, I asked Rafe if he'd stop the car near the river, just before the row of houses started.

Rafe waited in the car while I staggered out and down to the skiffs on the riverbank. It took me a little while to find the right Carrick cot that I'd thrown my bag into. I was shivering with cold when I pulled back a canvas cover and saw with great relief that my backpack was still safely stowed there. Soggy, but safe.

I was just about to haul it onto my back when a shot rang out. The sound sent a shockwave through my body.

My eyes darted up to the car.

I stumbled back up the hill to my uncle as fast as my legs would take me.

The driver's door was open.

I hurried around to the driver's side and fell to my knees in horror.

Rafe's body was lying half-out of the car. His head had fallen to the cobblestones, his neck was twisted, and his arms were hanging lifelessly from his body.

"Rafe!" I screamed, grabbing at him. "Rafe!" I screamed again, but he wouldn't respond.

I opened his coat, scared at what I would find.

I was dizzy. Everything was spinning.

All I could see was a big red blur.

He'd been shot in the chest.

Thudding feet approached me, and I shook my head, trying to focus.

"What's happened?" a voice cried.

"I heard a gunshot," cried another.

"Out of the way," said another, as I was suddenly pushed back by the small, pajama-clad crowd that had gathered.

Then I heard the two words I was dreading.

"He's dead."

31 DECEMBER

1 day to go . . .

12:50 pm

"Cal, you're OK!" cried Winter, as I opened my eyes. She was looking down at me—I was lying in a sleeping bag inside a tent.

"Where am I?" I asked.

"It's OK, you're safe. You've been unconscious for hours—since the travelers smuggled you back from the accident."

Winter said the last two words so softly, they were almost a whisper.

Everything flooded back to me. Rafe had been shot.

I couldn't speak. I was numb.

"I'm so sorry, Cal."

I shook my head and fought back tears.

"We wanted to go with him," cried Winter. "We wanted to help him find you, but he wouldn't let us—said it was too dangerous. I can't believe it. We only just saw him yesterday. He only just got here!"

A woman with hair even wilder than Winter's handed me a hot drink in a chipped mug and gently touched my shoulder.

Winter smiled at her gratefully.

Boges sat down beside me. "What happened?"

"He saved me," I said, finally finding my voice. "Sligo had thrown me in an oubliette—a deep dungeon. I was minutes from death, praying for the Ormond Angel to come and save me, and then Rafe appeared. It was a miracle. He drove us away—we were headed here—but I'd thrown my backpack into one of the cots by the river when Zombie Two was chasing me, so I asked him to pull over so I could get it. Then I heard a gunshot, ran back to the car and found him lying there . . . bleeding." I was dizzy again at the thought of him lying there so helplessly. "Locals started running over. I don't know what happened after that. I must have blacked out."

"You were practically frozen, Cal. You were in shock. You'd lost a lot of blood too. We're lucky to have you back so soon," said Winter.

There was a pause while we listened to the quiet gypsy camp around us. A fire crackled nearby, and I noticed a couple of scruffy kids looking our way, peering out from behind tent flaps.

"What about Mrs. Fitzgerald?" I asked.

"Mrs. Fitz was fine," Boges said. "We figured

we couldn't stick around. Not with the Garda asking questions. Winter stole—"

"Borrowed," she corrected him.

"*Borrowed* one of the travelers' horses, and when we came here to return it, they welcomed us in and offered us a place to sleep. Ashling and Quinn said we could stay as long as we wanted. They said they're always more than happy to help out good folk on the run from the Garda."

I was hearing some of what Boges and Winter were saying, but Rafe's face wouldn't leave my mind. I buried my head in my hands.

"What are we doing here?" I asked my friends. "People are dying! For what good reason? Why? For the sake of the Ormond Singularity? I don't even know if I can trust my own mother, so who am I doing this for? Why does it even matter anymore?"

"You have to keep going, Cal," insisted Winter.

"Why should I?"

"For the rest of your family. For Tom and Rafe. For your great-uncle. For your great-aunt." She stopped and shook her head. "For all the people who've helped you along the way—Jennifer Smith, Lachlan, Melba Snipe, Repro, Ryan Spencer, Nelson Sharkey. . . For us," she added, grabbing Boges's hand. "Me and Boges. We've both been here with you for almost all of this insane journey.

We believe in you. We want you to see it through to the end. If you quit now, everything will have been for nothing."

"You know she's right," said Boges. "Today's the last day, dude. You can't give up now. You have to keep it together for just a little bit longer."

My body was aching. Rafe's murder was consuming my thoughts, and the pressure of having only hours left was sending me into a sweat. But they were right. I had barely one more day to get through. A matter of hours to find the answers.

Everything Dad had left me was pointing to Inisrue Marsh. Was this where I'd find the ruin he'd photographed? Would there be an inscription around the walls, like we'd seen in the faded sketch?

For a moment I thought I could hear my dad's voice again, telling me to keep going. I had to find the Ormond Singularity. I *had* to.

"The map in the wardrobe pointed to Inisrue Marsh," said Boges. "Winter and I have directions. We're going there whether you want to or not, and we're going to find out why it was marked. Now, see if you feel strong enough to get up."

"OK," I said, as I began to shakily stand. "Did you just say you have directions?"

"Sure do, thanks to Ashling."

"Ashling?"

"The woman who brought you here," explained Boges. "She had a book, listing all of Black Tom Butler's land holdings in Inisrue in the sixteenth century. The bad news is that Inisrue is a swamp, but the good news is that it is home to the ruins of *three* of Black Tom's buildings—Slievenamon Castle, Cragkill Keep and Ormond Tower. One of them *has* to be the one your dad took the photos of. One of them *has* to hold the secret."

"I hope you're right," I said, feeling my strength returning.

"So do I," admitted Boges. "Winter made a copy of their location so we don't get lost."

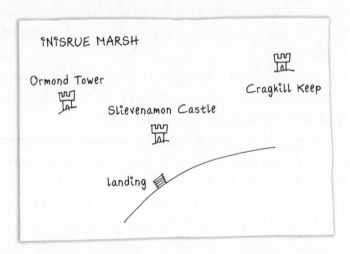

"The buildings were originally on an island in the middle of the river," Winter added, "but that was hundreds of years ago. They're still there, but now the island has turned into an unpredictable swampland. We'll have to be really careful."

"At least we don't have to worry about Rathbone anymore," I said. "Thanks to Sligo."

"What?" asked Winter suspiciously. "He killed him?" she guessed.

I nodded. "He said the bogs have already proven to be a great place for dumping a body . . ."

1:50 pm

My hands were sore, red and swollen from the failed attempts to climb the deadly spike, so Boges helped me slowly shuffle into warmer clothes. I was getting worried. We'd come all this way, I'd survived almost a year, despite the dangers of the Ormond Singularity. One of these ruins *had* to be the place.

I could feel Boges and Winter looking expectantly at me. Whether the ruins were rubble or not, we needed to search them.

"So we have three ruins to search," said Winter, as she shoved things back into her bag. "We have about ten hours left. Before midnight. Before the Ormond Singularity runs out."

"Even if we *do* find whatever the Ormond Singularity is before midnight," I said, "how do we prove it? There'll be no one there to witness it, except us."

"Relax, dude," said Boges. "I'll film it with my phone."

I was moving awkwardly, in pain as I gathered my things. I had been counting on everything falling magically into place over here, but I was still unsure of the basics. How was I going to clear my name?

I didn't see *Lives of the Saints* on the floor until I skidded on it, twisting my ankle and falling hard.

I yelped in pain. "Useless book!" I shouted, picking it up and throwing it at the wall of the tent. It made a slapping sound on the tarp-like fabric before hitting the ground.

"Take it easy," said Boges. He picked it up from the floor. "This is a valuable old book, man. *Was* a valuable old book," he corrected.

The cracked leather on the spine of the book had come apart, and the front cover was left hanging by a few threads.

I looked closer. Where the binding had come away from the book's spine, I could now see a narrow strip of vellum that had been wrapped around under it. Some kind of reinforcement for the stitching?

I snatched it from Boges and peered even

closer. The piece of vellum was familiar. It had been sewn into the underside of the cover, but was now loose because of the torn stitching.

Carefully, I pulled it out.

"Unbelievable," I breathed, mesmerized, smoothing it out.

"What is it?" Winter asked, coming over to see.

Slowly, I held up the piece of vellum.

Winter blinked, amazed. "It's the missing part of the Ormond Riddle! The last two lines!"

"Dude! Let me see!" said Boges, leaning over her shoulder, staring at the strip that I was holding up.

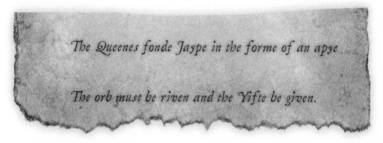

The Queenes fonde Jaype in the forme of an apye

The orb must be riven and the Yifte be given.

Winter read it out loud slowly, but instead of reading "yifte" she said, "gift."

"I can't believe it! Dr. Brinsley was right!" she said.

"But what does 'riven' mean?" I asked.

"I think it means 'split apart,'" replied Winter.

"Grab the rest of the Riddle," said Boges. "Let's put them both together."

The ORMOND RIDDLE

Eight are the Leaves on my Ladyes Grace

Fayre sits the Rounde of my Ladyes Face

Thirteen Teares from the Sunnes grate Doore

Make right to treadde in Gules on the Floore

But adde One in for the Queenes fayre Sinne

Then alle shall be tolde and the Yifte unfold

The Queenes fonde Jaype in the forme of an apye

The orb must be riven and the Yifte be given.

"'Apye,'" I quoted. "The form of an ape? The monkey! Winter! The white monkey in the portrait you saw of young Princess Elizabeth! It's holding an orb, and Dad drew a monkey holding a ball."

"I still don't get it," said Boges. "What does it mean? What's the 'Queenes fonde Jaype?'"

We both looked to Winter.

"Shakespeare uses that word," she said. "A 'jape' is a trick of some kind. A joke. Or some sort of deception. And in those days, the word 'fond' actually meant 'foolish.'"

"A foolish joke," I said, thinking aloud. "What do these last lines mean? Black Tom is supposed to have written these lines, according to Dr. Brinsley—what foolish joke is he playing?"

"Quick!" hissed Ashling, suddenly storming into our tent. "Get into the trailer, the Garda are here!"

"What?" I asked, panicking. "They're here?"

"You need to go and hide in the chests in the trailer. Now!"

Winter, Boges and I grabbed our bags and ran out of the tent, following Ashling into a trailer. Once inside, she started pulling books out of three separate chests, making room for us to climb inside.

"Get in!" she ordered.

The three of us awkwardly squashed ourselves

inside, then the heavy, dusty books were piled back on top of us.

"Don't move until I come back!" she hissed, before leaving.

2:27 pm

Cramped in a box of books, the minutes were flying by. Every minute passing meant less time and less daylight to get out to Inisrue Marsh and search the three potential locations.

Being found would hold us up at a time when *time* was as crucial as air. I was petrified we'd be caught by the Garda with our fake passports and be unable to answer their questions about Sligo's raid on the Clonmel Way Guest House the other afternoon . . . and about Rafe's body left lying in his car on the road.

I wondered if my mum had been notified yet. She'd be devastated. Again.

I also couldn't help thinking about what Rafe had told me before he died—about Mum's involvement with Rathbone.

At least for now it was quiet in the trailer. I hoped Boges and Winter were holding up in their hiding places OK.

2:38 pm

We were wasting so much time, and my body was

killing me. I couldn't help lifting the lid of the chest and peering out.

"Boges? Winter?" I hissed.

"Stay down," I heard Boges reply. "No point getting caught now. Surely they can't hang around for too much longer."

3:04 pm

"We just use this one as our library," I heard Ashling say as she entered the trailer, followed by heavy footsteps. "The children come in here to grab a book and study quietly."

"Uh-huh," an unknown voice replied, tapping what I suspected was a baton on top of the chests. "Books, you say," she added.

The sound of one of the chest lids opening sent chills down my spine. I heard some prodding and gritted my teeth, praying my friends weren't about to be spotted. I prepared myself to launch out of the chest and run, but in moments, Ashling and the unwanted guest had left the trailer. For good, I hoped.

3:20 pm

"It's OK, you can come out now," said Ashling, finally lifting up the lid on the chest I was in.

I stretched out my aching limbs and saw Boges and Winter also emerging, looking like disheveled, broken jack-in-the-boxes.

"I thought they'd never leave," said Ashling. "They were very thorough, investigating the Clonmel Way raid and the shooting. Checking our camp, making sure we weren't harboring any *fugitives*. Are you all right?"

Clearly, by the light-hearted way she said "fugitives," she thought we were kids who'd been caught up in the wrong place at the wrong time. If only she knew how serious this was.

"We're fine," I said. "Thank you for everything you've done for us, but we really need to get out of here. We must go to Inisrue Marsh."

Ashling shook her head. "I don't think you should set off now. It's far too dangerous to go there. There's not enough light, and you only have to wander a little way off the path, and you'll never be seen again. The Marsh has claimed a lot of lives over the years. Why don't you wait till morning? It'll be much safer then. You can stay here and celebrate the start of the new year with us!"

Morning would be too late, party or no party.

"What about by river?" I asked, thinking we could take one of the Carrick cots. "That would be safer, right?"

"It will take you longer, but it probably would be safer. Have you ever handled a boat?"

"Of course."

Ashling thought about it, then shook her head.

"You don't know how dangerous the bog lands can be," she said, trying again to talk us out of it.

"That won't be a problem," Winter interrupted confidently. "How will we know when we're nearing Inisrue Marsh?"

Ashling could see there was no point in trying to make us stay. "You head north from Waterford," she began, "and follow that direction for some time. When you reach the old St. Mullins Bridge—it has six stone arches—you'll know you haven't too much further to go. And when you're close to the marsh area, you'll find a stone landing. You can pull up the cot there."

"Thanks, Ash," I said, already out the trailer door and heading for the tent, while my friends rushed along behind me.

3:30 pm

"OK," I said, back in the tent. "Make sure you have everything."

"But we've gotta try the Caesar shift on the last two lines," said Boges.

I shook my head. "Not here, we don't have time. Let's do it on the way."

The flap on the tent was suddenly pulled

open once more. "Someone else is here!" shouted Ashling. We stopped dead. "Hide! There's no time to get you back into the trailer!"

I rushed to the opening to peer out. A huge wave of relief hit me when I saw who the camp intruder was.

"It's just Sharkey!" I said to my friends. Boges and Winter instantly relaxed. Winter even giggled. "He's with us," I explained to Ashling.

"Nelson!" I said, hurrying out to see him.

"Cal, my boy, I heard you had a close call last night. I'm so sorry to hear about your uncle," he said, uncomfortably stepping forward to give me a hug.

"Thanks," I said, awkwardly stepping out of his embrace. "We have to get going—we have three ruins to search, and time's almost out."

"I know, I know," Sharkey said.

Boges and Winter had joined us now. Boges shook Sharkey's hand, and Winter leaned in to give him a kiss on the cheek.

"I just wanted to let you know," continued Sharkey, "that I've spoken with Mrs. Fitzgerald from the guesthouse, and I am going to accompany her to the police station now. I feel confident she'll be able to identify Vulkan Sligo as her attacker. I also believe I have found something that will prove he was responsible for not only Theophilus

Brinsley's murder, but also your uncle's. I will do what I can to ensure he's found and arrested."

"You found something? Evidence?"

"Sure did," he replied. "Just call it the luck of the Irish."

"He murdered Sheldrake Rathbone too," I added. "Admitted it to me himself."

Sharkey exhaled loudly and cocked his head to one side before continuing. "The truth will come out, Cal. With Oriana de la Force behind bars, and only a matter of time before Sligo joins her, I promise your name will be cleared and you'll have your life back."

5:20 pm

Boges, Winter and I crouched low in one of the Carrick cots. We pushed it out in the icy water and paddled the narrow skiff along the river. The tide was behind us, helping us towards Inisrue Marsh.

It was well and truly dark, except for the glow of lights in the sky above a distant town, and the heavy-duty flashlight Boges had managed to borrow to help guide our way.

As soon as we'd settled into a steady rhythm, Winter began working on the Riddle by flashlight.

"I'll start with a one letter shift," she said, struggling to hold her pencil, paper, the Riddle and flashlight all at the same time. "I have a good feeling about this. A lot of trouble went into hiding these two lines—I'm sure they're going to tell us where to go next!"

As Winter worked, we glided past villages built along the watercourse and the wide barges moored beside them. Twinkling lights dotted some of the houses, reminding us again that it was New Year's Eve—a time for celebration. Rafe and I had both almost died on a small boat in Treachery Bay exactly one year ago. I didn't know if it was possible, but I could tell we were all silently hoping we'd be celebrating on the stroke of midnight too.

With a bit more luck, now that Nelson Sharkey was going to present evidence against him, the Garda would hunt Sligo down before the night was out. Then Winter at least, could resume a normal life, with him safely behind bars.

Further along, the tidal water rattled over the stones on the banks as we passed a small village and smelt the fragrant scent of wood fires burning in the cottages. Stars twinkled through clouds.

A milky mist hung over the water, and the sound of the tide moving to the coast was all I could hear. The skiff followed the course of the river. We couldn't really get lost—there was only *up* river or *down* river, and we knew we were heading in the right direction, looking out for the old St. Mullins Bridge.

A chill, different from the frosty air of the night, shivered through my bones, registering a sudden danger alert. I shuddered, uneasy. As the countdown to midnight ticked away, danger was increasing, tensing like a coiled spring.

"How are you doing, Winter?" I asked, as a distant town clock chimed six o'clock. We only had six more hours before the Singularity ran out, yet here we were, *still* trying to decipher the Riddle, when we had three locations to search. Three! Slievenamon Castle, Cragkill Keep and Ormond Tower.

The secret of the Ormond Singularity *had* to be in one of the ruins, but we didn't have time to search all of them.

Winter's voice interrupted my thoughts. "It's worrying me," she said, her face half-lit by flashlight. "This misspelling of 'ape.' I mean, I'd expect 'aype' just like in 'jaype,' not this 'apye' with the 'p' before the 'y.' Scribal errors happened in copied texts, but you wouldn't think it would happen in this Riddle. It's so obvious that it should be spelled the other way."

I caught a glimpse of Winter's face. She was smiling.

"What are you getting at?" asked Boges, pausing over his oar.

"What if it's *not* a scribal error?" I began, picking up Winter's excitement. "What if it was *deliberate*? Is that what you're saying? That the misspelling of 'apye' *is* the 'jaype' of the Riddle? Black Tom's *trick* is that word itself?"

"That's *exactly* what I mean!" Winter nodded vigorously. "That the error was made intentionally, so that the code would work! I'm going to check it right now!"

With the piece of vellum on her knees, Winter continued her decoding, focusing on the word "apye," starting as she'd begun with the first words, with just one shift along the alphabet.

"Don't forget," began Boges, breathlessly heaving on the oars, "to look for 'apye' in both lines of the alphabet. Apply it to the top line as well as the bottom line."

"You're right," said Winter. "It could go either way. I'll check both and see what they give us."

ABCDEFGHIJKLMNOPQRSTUVWXYZ

ZABCDEFGHIJKLMNOPQRSTUVWXY

"From the top line, 'apye' becomes 'zoxd,'" said Winter, shaking her head. "From the bottom line it becomes 'bqzf.' No good. I'll try two shifts along."

ABCDEFGHIJKLMNOPQRSTUVWXYZ

YZABCDEFGHIJKLMNOPQRSTUVWX

"OK, so with two shifts, from the top line, 'apye' becomes 'ynwc,'" she sighed. "From the bottom line it becomes—"

"It's 'crag!'" I yelled. "It's Cragkill Keep! Winter, you're brilliant! Maybe the 'double-key' code also hinted at the double shift needed to decipher 'apye!'"

"Careful," warned Winter, "you're going to tip over the boat!"

Winter wrote out the last of the letters, and now it was clear to see:

a – p – y – e

c – r – a – g

"Bridge coming up! Six arches!" yelled Boges triumphantly. "The St. Mullins Bridge! We're almost there!"

7:00 pm

Louder now, I could hear the clock chiming seven o'clock. We had five hours left to make it to Inisrue Marsh, find Cragkill Keep and search it. Winter's map showed that Cragkill was on the right of the stone landing.

Ignoring my stinging hands, I hauled on the paddles as Boges and I swung back and forward in long pulls, sending the light cot scudding up the river. Ahead, a low stone wall rose from the river bank, leading to a stone wharf.

"We're here," I said, swinging the skiff towards the banks. "This must be the landing Ashling told us about."

Inisrue Marsh

7:21 pm

We worked hard, cutting across the tidal surge, then jumped out, dragging the cot up onto the stones, running it aground.

Boges gasped at the cold, but I was too excited to even notice it myself.

We hauled ourselves up the bank and onto

the landing. A small, sinking stone house with darkened windows was the only intact building I could see, but just past it, blocking out the night sky ahead, was the looming mass of a great ruin.

"OK, we have to make our way along the bank to Cragkill Keep," said Boges, "which is further up on the right. Quick, follow me!"

Boges led the way with the sharp light from his flashlight.

Stay on the track, Ashling had warned. None of us wanted to end up sinking helplessly into the bog, like Rathbone had, but we dared to walk quickly along the narrow strip of firm, slightly raised ground that formed what we hoped was the safest path. On both sides of us, the quicksand of the marsh endlessly oozed into the dark, with only the occasional bare and struggling tree jutting out of its surface.

8:00 pm

The chiming clock, louder still, called out eight o'clock—it must have been in a nearby town. We'd been struggling along the muddy track through the marsh for over half an hour, and now we only had four hours left.

I paused. I'd heard something. I put up a hand to stop the others behind me.

Boges immediately doused his light. "What is it, dude?"

"Listen."

The darkness and silence of Inisrue Marsh surrounded us.

"What are we listening to?" whispered Winter.

"I don't know. But I get the feeling we're not the only people on this track."

I steadied myself and strained to listen again. "I think I can hear footsteps," I whispered, as quietly as possible. "Ahead of us, coming this way. Can you hear it?"

This time, the others heard it too.

Flickers of light from flashlights in the distance became visible ahead of us. Low voices drifted along the chilly air.

We crouched low, unsure of what to do and where to go. I didn't want to backtrack and lose ground, but I was worried we didn't have any other option. Winter suddenly gasped beside me—now footsteps seemed to be coming from behind us as well! We were stuck in the middle!

Not knowing who was closing in on us was the worst part. I couldn't even imagine who it could be; all I knew was that the intruders would be hostile. Hostile and desperate to stop us from uncovering the DMO first.

Then I recognized the loud voice ahead.

"*Sligo!*" Winter hissed, before I could.

What was he doing here? Wasn't he supposed to be in the hands of the Garda? If Sligo found us this time, we could kiss our lives and the Ormond Singularity goodbye forever.

"We have to get off the track!" I told my friends. "We can't let anyone see us!"

"Where should we go?" asked Boges. "We can't go into the bog—we'll be sucked down in seconds!"

Desperate, I swung around, trying to find a hiding place. Against the night sky, I spotted a gnarled and ancient-looking tree half-submerged in the marsh near the edge of the track a few yards ahead of us.

"That tree," I whispered to the others. "Let's climb in there and hide. Grab a branch and hang on for your lives. Whatever you do, don't let go—we have to stay above the surface."

The footsteps behind us crept closer.

I ran and leaped off the pathway, seizing the low branches of the ancient tree, throwing myself behind it while gripping it tightly with my raw hands.

Whack! Winter slammed into me as she did the same, almost making me lose my hold and my balance. Seconds later, Boges banged into us, almost sending both of us sprawling into the surrounding marshy mess.

I could already feel the mud closing over my feet. I hated to think what might happen if any of the branches snapped. I hung onto the bough even tighter than the day I was hanging from a tree with those dogs, Skull and Crossbones, snapping at my heels.

Boges and Winter were also straining to keep themselves up in the tree, the pained effort obvious in their shadowy faces.

"They haven't arrived yet," I heard Sligo say, as he wandered along the path nearby. "We can grab them and force that psycho kid into giving us the last piece of information. He won't be able to keep quiet if he has to watch you use your 'special techniques' on his stout friend and that repulsive little traitor! I know he'll talk if we grab them. And then we'll finally get rid of Ormond. For good, this time!"

Sligo must have returned to the empty oubliette and realized I'd escaped.

Tension choked the air as we huddled in the branches, trying to keep our nerves and chattering teeth under control.

The figures of Zombie Two and Sligo finally emerged from the murky air, mere yards away from where the three of us were clinging. They both stopped and stared into the darkness of the path leading back to the river.

"Vermin coming now, boss," Zombie Two growled. "I hear them coming."

Zombie Two clearly thought that it was me and my friends making our way down the track towards them. I held my breath.

The heavy pounding of whoever it *really* was who had been trailing behind us came closer.

A single silhouette, black and round, grew larger with every footstep. I knew that silhouette all too well.

I waited for him to step into the soft beam of moonlight that shone between him and the unsuspecting pair ahead on the path.

I heard a wheezing roar as Sumo suddenly became visible, head down on his massive chest, powerful arms raised in a fighter's stance. His flashlight pointed at Sligo and Zombie Two, standing side-by-side, who'd been expecting the three of us to appear, not Oriana's loyal sidekick.

Before Zombie Two and Sligo could react, Sumo doubled over and powerfully barreled into them both, knocking the wind out of them and sending them flying out over the marsh in a big black blur of tangled bodies!

The three wrestling bodies splashed into the treacherous swamp just feet from our unstable hiding place.

For a few seconds, they didn't realize the

serious danger they were in, and we heard them, shouting, struggling, swinging and kicking. Every twist, every turn, every defensive move was condemning them to a suffocating fate.

I should have known that Oriana's jail sentence wouldn't have meant the end of her pursuit of the Ormond Singularity. She must have sent Sumo to Ireland to finish what she'd started.

"C'mon," I said, trying to refocus. "Now's our chance to get out of here!"

I carefully swung myself out of the tree and planted my feet on firm ground. I held my arms out to help Winter and Boges to safety.

The shouts of the battling trio in the mud changed to cries of fear as they realized their threats were useless. They'd encountered an enemy that they couldn't beat—finally they were facing a force that was greater than all three of them combined.

"Help!" came Sligo's terrified voice. "Somebody help me! Please! Get me out of here!"

For a moment, Winter moved towards the bog, but both Boges and I stopped her. We weren't about to let the marsh take her too, for the sake of a man who'd tried to destroy her life. It was out of our hands now.

"Get off me!" shouted Sumo, from the darkness.

"Get off *me*!" shouted Zombie Two.

"Stop it, you fools!" cried Sligo. "You're both pushing me under!"

We could hardly see anything as they all sank lower and lower in the swamp, their struggles and violence only making it worse for them, quickening their relentless descent.

"There's nothing for us to see here. Let's go," I whispered to my friends. I took Winter's hand and led her away as the desperate cries from out of the unforgiving mud were slowly muffled . . .

And then even they were gone. There was nothing but silence behind us.

8:51 pm

We hurried along the final stretch, and my chest pounded harder with every step. Sligo had boasted about ridding himself of Rathbone in the mud, and now he had suffered the same demise. Maybe there was some kind of justice in the world.

I gripped Winter's hand firmly.

The silhouette of Cragkill Keep finally emerged from the dark, wet mass of Inisrue Marsh. At one time, I guessed, the river would have flowed close to the Keep, but now it was a hundred yards or so away.

9:00 pm

The clock sounded over Cragkill Keep, reminding

us that we had only three hours to go. The Keep stood alone in a field, its fragmented shape etched against the rising half-moon sky. Even by moonlight, and despite the whorls of mist around its crumbling towers, I recognized the ruin from the photos on my dad's memory stick.

We moved our flashlights over the stone ruin. Only the central section of the building remained partly intact, with crumbling towers at each end like a giant's four-poster bed.

"No!" said Boges, as our flashlight also revealed that Cragkill Keep was completely surrounded by a tall security fence and locked double gates. Inside this compound I could see earthmoving equipment—a huge bulldozer and two cranes sitting idle. We were locked out. "Man, what's all this about?" asked Boges. "Why is it fenced off like this?"

The huge bulldozer with its immense jaw-like scoop squatted on a rise a little way from the massive ruin, next to what looked like flood lights. Piles of numbered stones were stacked nearby, awaiting transportation.

I turned to Boges and Winter. "Mrs. Fitzgerald said that one of the ruins here was being boxed up and shipped back to the USA."

"It *would* have to be this one," said Winter in frustration. "What if somebody has already stumbled on the Ormond Singularity? What if they've already been in there and taken it?"

"Don't panic. We should know by now that the Ormond Singularity isn't something that people can just 'stumble on,'" said Boges. "I don't think it'd just be sitting in there waiting for someone to walk in and find it."

"I know that," Winter said. "But they might have been digging around. They might have accidentally lucked onto it."

"Come on, guys," I said, mentally measuring the height of the wire mesh. "What's a little fence between us and the Ormond Singularity? We're going over."

I threw my backpack over the fence and bit down on my flashlight, ready to scramble up and over the security fence.

"What about this?" asked Winter, pointing to a small sign.

WARNING!

FOLEY SECURITY, WATERFORD

Back-to-base electronic surveillance

UNAUTHORIZED PERSONS KEEP OUT!

YOU ARE BEING MONITORED ON OUR SURVEILLANCE SYSTEM

"I can't see any cameras anywhere, can you?" I said, jumping the fence and landing on the other side.

Winter followed me, throwing her bag over the tall wire netting and throwing herself up on it.

Finally, Boges took a running jump and threw himself up and over the fence too. He dropped to the ground on the other side, puffing.

9:33 pm

The three of us stood inside the grounds, examining the decaying ruin. Weeds grew wildly through cracks in the rubble and over large blocks of stone. We navigated around them, stepping cautiously through the wet grass, avoiding tripping on the uneven ground.

Starry sky peered eerily through the empty window arches of a collapsed tower. Dead grass and plants speared out of the broken walls. The second, less damaged tower stood opposite the first, and I could just make out some kind of statue standing on a perch within it.

"What is that?" Winter asked.

Eroded and hidden by the jut of a stone corner, the figure was impossible to make out.

"Not sure," I said, pointing my flashlight through an archway to the interior.

Some of the original roofing remained at the

furthest end, and this had protected a section of the stone flooring of what I guessed would have once been the Keep's great hall.

A tremor of fear and apprehension filled me. I couldn't shake the feeling that even though Oriana, Rathbone, Sligo, Zombie Two and Sumo were out of the picture, trouble was very close. We were right where we were supposed to be, I reminded myself. Cragkill Keep. The worst thing that could happen was that we'd run out of time.

Winter guided her light along the mossy stone walls of the interior and up to the sections of the first-floor roof that still remained. Remnants of the plaster patterns that had once decorated the ceiling were now stained and broken, with dead vines drooping from them.

I lowered my flashlight, moving it over the uneven floor of the long room. Under the debris and dead leaves, I could see the remains of mosaic tiling.

"What are we even looking for?" Boges asked the question we were all thinking.

"We won't know what we're looking for until we find it," I said.

10:00 pm

I started panicking as the distant chimes called out again. We had two hours to midnight.

"Spread out," I urged, "and look for anything that might give us a clue. Anything familiar."

After a lot of frantic searching, we all stopped and stared back at each other hopelessly. Was this the end of the road? Had we reached another dead end?

"Come over here!" Winter suddenly shouted. "Look at this!"

Boges and I hurried over to her. She was shining her flashlight down to where the corners of a huge fireplace met the broken stone of the floor. There was something carved on the stone. It was small and worn by the weather.

"It's a rose!" I said, squatting beside it. "Like that one in the drawing of the little kid!" My heart beat a little faster. "And look! Just above it!"

"The pattern on Gabbi's ring," said Winter, pointing to the silver ring on my finger. "The Carrick bend design!"

Just above the rose, the Carrick bend had been carved along the stone wall. It too, was eroded and almost invisible.

"Maybe the rose means something like 'X marks the spot,'" I said hopefully. I shone my flashlight up and around, searching the darkness in the corner under the collapsing roof.

You were here, Dad, I thought to myself. You knew something was here. You noticed something—why can't I see it? *What were you trying to tell me?*

As I strained to make out more of the rotting designs in the crumbling plaster, brilliant lights suddenly came on, flooding the interior of the ruined Keep.

Boges and Winter blinked in astonishment, quickly turning around, bracing themselves.

I freaked out. It was now as bright as day. Who was here?

"Get out of sight!" I ordered, ducking into the narrow corridor we'd first come through and peering around the corner of the wide archway.

Someone had switched on the flood lights. I could hear the generator humming outside.

As I crouched out of the light, I nearly jumped out of my skin as some huge piece of machinery revved into life outside. I craned my neck further around the corner. Some distance away, near the fence line, the massive bulldozer we'd seen earlier had come to life! A hunched figure sat at the controls.

I raced back to the others. "We have to hurry. If we stay out of sight, the guy in the bulldozer might not even realize we're in here. Looks like he's loading stones onto a pallet or something."

"At this hour?" Winter asked. "Nearly midnight? On New Year's Eve?"

"I've heard of overtime," said Boges, "but that's crazy."

The bright light shone on the stained and discolored plaster of the ceiling above the corner, and for the first time I could see traces of words. As more of the damaged plaster of the corner came into focus, I gasped.

AM R ET   VRE
TOSJO S CEL R

"Wow!" yelped Boges, over the sound of the bulldozer, following my line of sight and spotting the words on the wall. "The words inscribed on the Ormond Jewel!"

"And look up here! You can see where they are repeated high up on the wall!" cried Winter, carefully stepping across the uneven floor to see the faint words better. "They would have run all the way around this section of the gallery! Just like in the old sketch you found in Dr. Brinsley's study!"

The spot we were standing in looked like it had once been a small room, just off the main, long gallery.

"Now I *know* we're in the right place," said Winter. "Even in the right corner! The rose and inscription are showing us the way!"

My exhilaration surged as did the sense of danger. I was *shaking* with mixed emotions. To be so close . . . so close to *what?*

Boges twisted to look at the roof and tripped over something on the floor. The contents of his backpack flew out, and his water bottle hit the ground, popping its lid and spraying water everywhere.

Winter went to help him gather up his things, retrieving his bottle. Most of the water had spilled out onto the ground, making a slippery mess on the mud-covered mosaic flooring.

"Hey, look at this—there's some kind of pattern on these tiles," said Winter, squatting down to take a closer look. "Underneath the dirt."

"We don't have time for appreciating tiles," said Boges, getting back on his feet.

"You'd better make time for this," scoffed Winter, her voice quivering with excitement. "Cal, get over here and check this out!"

She dropped to her hands and knees and wrenched off her scarf, scrubbing the ground with it. She grabbed Boges's bottle and splashed more water over the tiles. "Don't just stand there, help me!"

We joined her and started clearing more of the tiles—me with my bare hands, Boges with his beanie—pushing aside leaves and debris, wiping dirt away.

Outside, the bulldozer seemed to be getting louder.

"Luckily they're only here to dismantle the place," Boges said, "not destroy it."

I stood back up, shining my flashlight onto the area we'd been working on. Although smeared and dirty, parts of the original mosaic floor of the gallery started to become clear. More and more was being revealed with every sweep of Winter's wet scarf.

"Get up!" I shouted excitedly to my friends. "Look!"

A pattern in the tiles, of intertwined leaves of faded yellow, surrounded what once would have been a huge, dark green oval. I dug around in my backpack and pulled out the Ormond Jewel, holding it up over the remnants of the pattern on the floor.

There was no doubt about it.

"It's the same design as the front of the Ormond Jewel! The Ormond Jewel is a *miniature*!

It's a tiny replica of the floor design of Cragkill Keep!"

Stunned by this revelation, the three of us stood immobilized, staring at each other, then at the tiled jewel on the floor beneath us.

Feverishly we dropped back to our knees, to clear more of the rubble and grass, revealing more patches of colored tiling.

"Look!" I said. "There's the pattern of red and white tiles! The same pattern as the alternating rubies and pearls surrounding the emerald!"

Little by little, the clues were falling into place!

"Hurry," I said to the others. "If that guy in the bulldozer comes any closer, he'll spot us. We mustn't be seen. The clock's ticking!"

I could hear Winter reciting the words of the Ormond Riddle under her breath as she cleared enough ground to start examining the alternating red and white tiles.

"There are thirteen white tiles," she said. "The same number as the pearls on the Ormond Jewel."

"Thirteen teares, thirteen tiles, thirteen steps!" said Boges excitedly. "The numbers in the Riddle relate to counting out the steps on this floor!" Boges suddenly stopped, looking deflated. "But the thirteen steps we need to take have to start from 'the Sunnes grate Doore,'" he said.

"Is there some sort of grate or door around here? I can't see anything like that."

With the grinding of the bulldozer becoming louder, I risked running down to the other end of the gallery and back again.

"There's nothing on the floor near the arch where we came in," I reported.

"We don't need to look for a grate," said Winter. "That's just old-fashioned spelling for 'great.' We should be looking for something big that lets the sun in—a *great* door or something."

I looked around. "'The Sunnes grate Doore,'" I repeated.

A mix of moonlight and floodlight shone on the rough floor of the ruin. I tried to follow the beams of moonlight and imagined sunlight pouring through the gaping arches of the three-tiered window in the tower rearing above us.

A wave of vibrations shuddered through the stone walls as the rumbling from the big earthmover outside became louder. What was left of the roof of the main gallery trembled visibly.

"Something that lets the sun in?" said Winter, suddenly beside me. She was looking up at the moonlight, like me—at the crumbling arches of the empty windows.

"Them?" I asked, staring at the arches. "The

sun would have come streaming through those windows. Onto the floor. Just like the moonlight is trying to do now!"

Winter raced over to the crumbling stones beneath the ruined windows and stood there directly against the wall. "If we take the thirteen steps as starting from here, under the big triple window—the sun's great door—we might find something."

I ran over to join her, and we walked the steps, counting aloud over the drone of the bulldozer.

One, two, three, four, five, six, seven, eight, nine, ten, eleven, twelve, thirteen... We could go no further. We had already come up hard against the opposite wall of this smaller, ruined room we were in. I stood there with my nose almost touching the cold stone wall as disappointment drained me.

There was nothing beyond the thirteenth step.

"The tiles don't lead anywhere," I said bitterly. "They end right here at this wall. It's not working. The Riddle isn't right!"

"'Thirteen Teares from the Sunnes grate Doore,'" Winter chanted, "'Make *right* to treadde in Gules on the Floore . . .'"

I paused. "Make *right*!" I shouted. "I've gotta take a step to the *right*."

"Of course!" cried Winter.

I stepped to the right and kicked away the leaf litter and debris at my feet.

"You're standing on a red tile!" said Boges. "'*Gules!*' Gules means red! Gules on the floor!"

"But there's only one of them! Hard up against the wall!" I said.

At that moment, the sound of the bulldozer outside roared at top speed, and the wall under the gaping hole of the ruined window started to crack in a thin, jagged black line.

Boges yelled. "We'll have to show ourselves, dude. That guy's going to kill us!"

"We can't!" I said. "We're so close to the deadline!"

"You have to 'adde One in, for the Queenes fayre Sinne,'" recited Winter, who seemed unaware of the danger we were in. "That means there should be one more tile! There should be *two* red tiles. The Riddle says so!"

"But there's only one here," I argued.

"Can we have this conversation somewhere else please, dudes?" yelled Boges, over the noise of the bulldozer outside. "That crack's getting bigger every second! The wall's going to fall, and we're going to be crushed!"

He was right. The crack in the wall now ran all the way down from the window and almost the entire length of the gallery. It was getting wider, deeper and blacker the longer I stared at it.

A shower of small stones from around the three-tiered window above dropped dangerously close. It was about to come down. The entire Cragkill Keep was about to come down.

As I stood there, immobilized with frustration, unwilling to just walk away from the Ormond Singularity, the other wall next to me cracked wider with a sound like a gunshot.

Bigger stones tumbled and crashed to the ground, peppering me with stinging fragments.

"Cal!" urged Boges. "I'm serious, we have to move! We have to get out of here!"

"We can't," cried Winter. "We can't leave now! We're so close! There's gotta be something else. The Riddle talks about the orb being riven and the gift being given. Something's wrong! Where's the orb?"

Boges grabbed me and Winter by the arms. "You betcha something's wrong! A lunatic in a bulldozer's bringing the house down around us! We'll be flattened if we don't get out now!"

Everything was trembling violently. Boges's fingers dug into my upper arm, wrenching me away from the wall.

"Come *on*! This whole place is about to come

down on top of us!"

"No! We can't leave now!" insisted Winter, a crazed, fearless determination in her eyes. "If we leave now, the Ormond Singularity is lost. Cal will never find out what it is!"

The crack in the wall next to me suddenly shifted, and another ominous zigzag crack appeared, spearing down its entire length. More stones and rocks cascaded down.

"Watch out!" I lunged at Winter, knocking her out of the way as a huge rock fell, narrowly missing her.

The close call shook me out of my stupor. Boges was right. "We'll die if we don't get out now!" I shouted.

"That's what I've been trying to tell both of you!" screeched Boges.

I grabbed Winter's arm and pulled her along, following Boges. We were about to run across the shaking floor and get outside, when a huge crash made me turn back to see the wall I'd been facing moments ago collapsing. If we'd still been standing there, we would have been crushed by its bulk. Like a line of dominoes, the length of the wall crumpled in a cloud of dust.

And then something amazing happened . . .

The collapsed wall revealed a black cavity behind it.

"It was a false wall!" Winter shouted. She too had stopped to witness the collapse. "That's why the tile steps suddenly stopped. See? There's a space behind it!" She ran back through the dust cloud to peer into the space that had opened up—it was about the size of a backyard shed. "And there's the other red tile! See? Just here, where the wall was stopping us before! I *told* you there'd have to be another one. The Riddle said so!"

Winter pointed, and another huge rock fell from above and shattered on impact just inches from her. It sent up more murky dust, acting like a smokescreen.

I heard Boges shout as he was struck by something on the side of the face.

Now we really did have to run for our lives. I thought I heard the clock chiming again—eleven o'clock—but I couldn't tell over all the rumbling and panic.

I grabbed Winter's arm once more and started dragging her out. But as I dodged another rock crashing close behind us, I caught a glimpse of something colorful within the dark cavity. Something on the floor, just beyond the last of the red tiles.

I squinted. Protected for centuries from the elements by the fake wall, was a perfect mosaic!

In it was a white monkey holding a ball—an orb—just like the monkey in Dad's drawing!

"Boges, Winter! Wait! Look!"

As my friends and I stood mesmerized by the amazing tiled image, the floor cracked before our eyes, and the monkey mosaic began to destruct. The mosaic was buckling up and then collapsing apart, like in an earthquake.

"It's a prophecy!" cried Winter. "The whole thing's breaking up!"

"The orb must be riven," I whispered, stunned, as the image of the white monkey holding the orb seemed to lift up momentarily then subside, breaking up and draining downwards in a waterfall of puzzle pieces. It vanished into the darkness under the floor like it was being swallowed by a sinkhole.

Masonry and stones pelted down around us, while outside, the bulldozer revved again, making another assault on the surrounding walls, attacking what little remained of the structure.

Fearfully, we made our way to the edge of the hole that was getting larger by the second. More and more of the floor collapsed and disappeared into the cavity.

Any moment, I thought, we would join the rest of the floor and be sucked down into the darkness of the foundations of the Cragkill Keep. Then suddenly, the sound of the bulldozer stopped.

The shower of rocks and stones eased.

The floor movements shuddered to a halt.

I seized the opportunity and crept right up to the widening hole and peered into it.

Under the piled-up earth and broken tiles, I could see the corner of a wooden chest.

Boges and Winter teetered over beside me, dodging falling debris.

"Dude, that must be the treasure!" Boges shouted.

With that, the three of us reached in and started digging away like mad dogs, trying to free the wooden chest from the rubble that had fallen in on top of it.

11:08 pm

"Cal?" came a voice, approaching from outside. "Cal, are you in there?"

"Sharkey!" Boges shouted out. "We're over here! Come and see what we've found!"

Nelson appeared in the crumbling archway.

He strode over, looking up and around, overwhelmed by the disaster zone inside the Keep. "I've stopped that crazy guy in the bulldozer, but this place is dangerously unstable. You need to get out."

As he spoke, a huge stone from the top of the wall crashed down behind him, making us all jump.

Sharkey stopped when he saw what we were all staring at. He whistled. "Seems like you've found what you were looking for!"

"We found it, all right!" I said, almost exploding with excitement. "Can you give us a hand?" I asked, indicating the pile of rubble in the cavity under the floor. Adrenaline was surging through every muscle in my body, making me shiver uncontrollably.

Eventually the four of us were able to haul the extremely heavy chest up.

Puffing and panting, we dropped it near the archway. As it settled on the ground, one side of the ancient wooden box split open, and a stream of gold spilled out! A steady flood of golden coins, lit by the brilliant generator lights, kept spreading in a gleaming pool!

It was like a dream come true. I could feel the excitement of the others. I realized I had a huge grin on my face.

Another heavy stone from the ceiling crashed straight into the top of the chest, splitting the lid into jagged pieces, sending more gold and precious jewels cascading out.

We all stepped back, speechless. Through the

split wood I could see the gleam of gold, the flash of colorful gems, and what looked like an ancient document, partly obscured by the broken rock. But before we did anything else, I needed proof. If the contents of this chest turned out to be the Ormond Singularity, I needed proof that I'd found it before the deadline. Before time was up at midnight on December 31st.

"Boges!" I said, turning to them all. "We did it! Get the camera out and start filming!"

"While you're doing that," said Sharkey, "I'll get some big canvas sacks I have in the back of my car."

I barely heard his words as I threw off bits of the broken rock and splintered wood until the contents of the chest were plain to see: a collection of amazing jewels and gold coins, gold chains, ropes of pearls and, most importantly, the signed document that sat on the top of it all.

"We did it!" I yelled again. I threw my arms around my friends, and the three of us jumped around with excitement. "Let's look at what we've discovered!"

My hands were trembling as I carefully lifted out the document. I knew from the touch that it was vellum. I smoothed it open so Boges could film it more easily.

Codicil: The Ormond Singularity

I give you this charge, my beloved 'black husband', as I gave
you the charge years ago when our honest nurse and
servant, Kat, conveyed to you, with utmost secrecy, the
gracious fruit of 'amor et suevre tosjors celer'.

I trust you will not be corrupted by any manner of gift, and
that you will be faithful with respect of our declaration of
mutual and eternal secrecy. I am already bound to a husband,
which is the kingdom of England. For me, this end must be
sufficient: that a marble stone shall declare that a Queen,
having reigned such a time, lived and died childless.

Therefore I charge you to guard our own great secret work,
and do assign these rights, privileges and titles to that same
secret. This is to be known henceforth as the Ormond
Singularity, benefiting the male line of Piers Duiske, so
that he and his heirs shall never be wanting.

By the love you bear his mother, when he attains his
majority, give him this mantle of black velvet, well-jewelled,
and this psalter, broidered by my own hand, complete with
rights, privileges and titles as set out herein.

Given under our signet at our honour
at Hampton Court, 1573

The Queen and Black Tom had a baby together. A baby who no one could know about.

Carefully, I picked up a small book from the chest. The cover was decorated with colored silk stitching. Flowers, Tudor roses and tiny pearls were woven around the initial "E" on the cover.

"Hey!" I said, recognizing it. "We've seen this before—in that portrait you discovered, Winter, in the Sotheby's catalog. Hanging from her waist in the painting."

I put it down, my attention taken by something else. Tucked down beside the pile of gold coins lay an embroidered leather satchel. Carefully, I opened it. It contained something made of really fine material, embroidered with pearls and gold. I picked it up. For a few seconds it hung in my hands—a precious silky robe, made for a tiny baby. But then it fell into shreds, dropping away from my hands into dusty fragments.

"The silk has perished!" cried Winter. "What a shame! But look at the beautiful trimming! How sad for the princess—and later the queen. She could never acknowledge her baby. She'd have been in huge danger if people ever found out. She would have been killed over it. And look at this!" she said, picking up another locket. "It's a bit like the Ormond Jewel!"

She passed it to me. The locket, with a yellow

crystal surrounded by diamonds and gold on its top lid, opened to reveal a miniature of Princess Elizabeth on one side and on the other, a portrait of a boy, holding a rose.

"The boy with the rose," breathed Winter. "Like your dad's drawing!"

"The boy," I repeated. "It wasn't just the secret love between Black Tom and Princess Elizabeth. The *greater* secret love was their son—the child they had together."

Winter attempted to pick up the shreds of rotted yellow silk, gathering them into her hands together with the embroidered borders of gold and pearls. "Elizabeth made this for her baby. The baby she could never share with the world. She was the 'great unknown lady' who sadly couldn't name herself."

"This little guy is the reason for the Ormond Singularity. He grew up and became Piers Duiske Ormond. All this," I said, pointing to the treasure trove and documents signed by the Queen, "was supposed to be claimed by Piers Duiske Ormond, for his family and his heirs, but something happened and it was never retrieved. Maybe his dad, Black Tom, died without ever revealing where it was hidden exactly. We'll never know why it wasn't claimed. The descendants of Piers Duiske Ormond kept the line going. The line that started with Black Tom and Princess Elizabeth. My ancestor, Piers Ormond, was gathering information about this secret when the Great War interrupted him. Dad took over and somehow got hold of the Ormond Jewel, but then he got sick and . . ." My voice trailed away. I hoped that somewhere, somehow, my dad could see what I'd done and be happy about it.

"The line came right down to you," said Winter. "It would have all belonged to your dad if he'd lived—he was the older twin. But now it falls to you. You're the older twin. It's been here for centuries, just waiting for whoever could decipher the Ormond Riddle and read the Ormond Jewel."

I wanted to say something, but it was hard to talk. Thoughts of Dad and Rafe were making me simultaneously overjoyed and sad.

A shower of stones reminded me that the situation here was pretty dicey. We needed to get this gear secured somehow and then get out.

"How much do you think all this is worth?" wondered Boges, his eyebrows almost jumping off his forehead with excitement.

"Millions," answered Sharkey, who had reappeared, carrying some big canvas bags. "At least. Something like this," he said, coming closer to look at the book, "is worth a fortune in itself. The Queen embroidered it with her very own initial."

"What about all these parchments written in Latin?" asked Winter. "The titles and deeds to different properties?"

"Millions more," said Sharkey. "Enough talk. Start loading everything into these bags."

I straightened up, puzzled at the change in the tone of his voice.

"Shouldn't we call the authorities?" I said. "I want to do this properly. I've discovered the Ormond Singularity before the deadline, and I want this acknowledged. All legal and above board."

Boges and Winter nodded in support.

"We can do all that in the morning," said Sharkey. "As soon as the banks open, you should deposit all this. You won't be able to take it out of the country without Customs clearance. In the meantime, we really just need to secure it all."

"I guess you're right," I said, but deep down inside me, I couldn't help thinking *something was wrong. Danger was close.*

Nelson gave each of us one of the bags, and we started loading them up with the contents of the treasure chest. I filled my bag with the heaviest stuff first—gold coins and chains. On top of that I placed ropes of pearls and shining rings, and then finally, I added the book and the embroidered leather satchel with the Ormond Singularity inside.

"OK," said Sharkey, holding his canvas bag into which he'd just squeezed one huge ruby ring before securing the flaps. By the time our four bags were filled and sealed, there wasn't much left at the bottom of the crumbling wooden chest. The rest we could get later. "OK," repeated Sharkey, "let's load up my vehicle."

With the walls still shaking around us and stones crashing down, we staggered with the weight of the treasure in our bags, and finally, the four of us emerged from the ruins of Cragkill Keep. We continued across the uneven ground to where Sharkey had parked his rented pickup truck—he'd driven right over a section of the wire fencing.

I noticed that the bulldozer was sitting quietly nearby.

"What was that?" asked Winter, pointing into the distance in the direction of the bog that had taken Sligo, Zombie Two and Sumo. "I just saw someone over there!"

"I think I saw it too," added Boges. "Movement over by that tree. You don't think one of them could possibly have—"

"Come on, let's get this stuff into the pickup already," said Sharkey, swinging his own bag into the bed.

We heaved our bags into the bed, and Sharkey quickly roped them down. Once everything was loaded up, the three of us climbed inside the cab and squashed up together, waiting for Sharkey to take his place behind the wheel.

I sat back, exhausted and happy.

Winter sat between Boges and me and gripped our hands tightly. We couldn't believe it. We had cracked the mystery of the Ormond Singularity.

All that remained now was bringing it home safely and getting our lives back.

11:32 pm

The driver's door swung open, and we waited for Sharkey to climb in. I looked back at the ruin, grateful for everything it had given us. Then I turned around and realized I was facing the snub of an automatic pistol.

It was pointed at me.

"Nelson, what are you doing?" I asked, thinking this was some sort of sick joke.

"Get out. All of you," he ordered, gesturing with the pistol. "Right now."

"What?" came Boges's shocked cry.

"Nelson?" Winter demanded. "What are you doing? What's going on?"

He didn't answer, just menaced us again with the business end of the pistol.

"Do as I say. Get out. *Now!*"

I was too stunned to move immediately.

"Do as I say, or I'll fire."

Fire? At us?

"But, Sharkey—" I began, completely shocked and confused.

Slowly my brain registered what was going on. I was furious at myself for not having seen it sooner. It had been there all along, and I hadn't seen it!

Rathbone's list.

Deep Water. *Sharkey. Sharks swim in deep water!*

Nelson Sharkey was "Deep Water!"

"You pretended to be on our side!" I shouted at him, pushing my friends out of the pickup and standing in front of them. "All this time you were lying to us! Pretended to help, and now you are completely betraying us!"

Rage was gushing up through my spine, shooting down into my arms and fingers. My fists were ready to strike out.

Another vicious movement from the gun stopped me in my tracks.

"Don't do anything stupid, Cal. Just do what I say. You too," he said, gesturing the gun in

Winter and Boges's direction. "It's turned out just as I hoped it would. All I had to do was tag along, lend a hand so I'd earn your trust, and ride your coattails until you tracked down the secret of the Ormond Singularity for me."

"But Sligo? You said you had proof!"

Sharkey laughed. "Proof? How could I have proof? Just add it to the list of lies you fell for," he scoffed. "And Sligo didn't shoot your uncle, *I* did!"

Anger surged through me. He killed my uncle! I picked up a rock and pelted it at him.

He deftly ducked it, standing upright again with a crooked smile.

"But your kids? Your old job? Was none of it true?" pleaded Winter.

"I hate kids! I don't have any offspring skipping around. I don't have an ex-wife, either!"

"But what about the reunion?" Winter continued, tears streaming down her face.

Sharkey laughed again. "I've been here following you three this whole time—I don't have family in Dublin! I haven't been at a reunion! I'm not even Irish!" He shook his head and grinned. He was enjoying this. "I *was* a detective, I didn't lie about that. I had quite an undercover money ring going until my partner in crime—that she-devil Oriana de la Force—hung me out to dry. We could have been an incredible pair."

"What about the clover?" Winter pleaded. "We thought you cared about us . . ."

"Nice touch, eh," scoffed Sharkey. "It had a tracking device in it! I was particularly proud of that one."

"Brinsley?" I asked tentatively.

"Old fool wouldn't give me what I needed."

"You killed him? But I—"

"But, but, but," mocked Sharkey.

Every lie, every reveal, every betrayal hit me in the gut, hard. Desperately I looked at my friends. Winter looked heartbroken; Boges looked ready to attack.

"The passports," whimpered Winter, "the clover . . . It was all just to fool us. How could you?" she asked him. "We *trusted* you."

"That was the idea," Sharkey scoffed, before forcing us at gunpoint back to the Keep, back through the archway and into the central gallery.

From the corner of my eye, I noticed that the light in the bulldozer had come on again.

"How many lives does that guy have?" Sharkey muttered to himself, looking back and noticing it too. "I should have hit him harder. He thinks he can pay me to do all his dirty work, and then he can take all the glory! Not a chance!"

Who was Sharkey talking about?

I had discovered the truth of the Ormond Singularity before midnight, December 31st, and I had the proof of this on Boges's cell phone, but none of that mattered if Nelson Sharkey was about to get away with my colossal inheritance.

It was just the three of us now. Mum, Gab, me. I needed all of the treasure so I could get my family back to where we were before. Buy back our house, buy back our old lives.

With a last flourish of the pistol, Sharkey cornered us, then ran back to his pickup. We glared at him in disbelief as he climbed into the cab in the distance and revved up the car. Mud skidded out from underneath the tires.

The three of us slumped with desolation. We felt destroyed.

All of a sudden, the bulldozer thundered and charged into view, scoop raised high.

Stunned into silence, we watched as the bulldozer drove right up to Sharkey's pickup, blade hovering directly above the driver's seat.

"What's going on?" screeched Boges, breaking the spell of silence. "Sharkey's about to get flattened!"

We heard Sharkey's horrendous howling before the bulldozer shifted gears, sending the menacing, heavy scoop pounding down on top of him, crushing the entire front end of the pickup like a half-squashed bug.

"He's dead for sure," said Boges, in a daze. "Sharkey's dead."

"Who's driving that thing?" asked Winter, completely bewildered.

"I don't know," I said. I couldn't believe what we'd just witnessed. "It must have been someone who knew Sharkey was a bad guy. Let's go find out."

But as we ran towards the bulldozer, the driver revved it up, lowered its huge blade, and came straight at us, lights blazing.

"Hey!" yelled Boges, as we scrambled backwards. "Stop! What do you think you're doing?"

Winter ran over to the cab, reaching up to bang on the glass, but the crazy driver paid no attention and continued powering straight towards the archway—and me and Boges!

If he took the archway out, I knew that the teetering tower nearby would come tumbling down in an avalanche, with all of us under it!

"Hey! Stop!" I yelled, waving my arms madly in the headlights.

I knew he couldn't hear me over the noise of the big earthmover, but I was right in his line of sight. Surely he could see me. I came closer, waving my arms. Boges and Winter joined me, flapping and shouting.

"He's not going to stop!" I shouted. "He's trying to kill us too! We'll have to run!"

It was then that the driver put his head out of the cab, revealing his identity . . .

But it couldn't be!

He was dead!

I'd seen him slumped, lying half-out of the car. I'd seen the bullet wound.

Then I saw his grin.

Him!

Had it all been staged?

It was as if the world stood still, and a whole lot of loose strands that had been twisting and turning in my mind suddenly fused together. The bulldozer revved up again, and despite the falling shower of stones, I had a moment of diamond clarity.

As I focused on his determined face, the smell that I'd been trying to remember came clearly into my mind.

It wasn't Mum's perfume.

It was the pungent smell of cigars.

I realized who had been behind almost every bad thing that had happened since the crazy guy, Eric Blair, had tried to warn me last year.

I now knew the identity of my archenemy.

He was coming at me, deliberately targeting the wall, intending to push the whole ruin down on top of us. With the speed of light, the missing pieces in my mind slotted into place.

My enemy was an ex-botanist whose special area of interest was the *toxins found in bracken ferns*. I recalled skimming through the boxes of botanical textbooks and notes in his office.

Mrs. Fitzgerald thought Dad had been acting strange the night she'd interrupted him at the Clonmel Way Guest House, unexpectedly cooking up some rotten-smelling herbal stew.

Except it hadn't been Dad at all. Someone else had opened that door. *Someone else who looked exactly like my father.*

Was he preparing the nerve toxin to give to my dad and his friend Eric Blair? Either secretly placed in food they would eat, or more brazenly, at a friendly meal for the three of them?

Rafe.

Rafe had flown to Ireland while telling us he was on vacation out of state. *He'd* impersonated my dad at the guesthouse, brewing up a toxin to poison his brother.

A poison that destroyed Dad's brain, mimicking a virus. That was what Dad had been trying to tell me all the time—he'd been trying to warn me against his own brother. *Rafe.*

My uncle. My dad's twin. *Double Trouble.* The last of the nicknames.

Rafe's head disappeared back into the cab, and the bulldozer accelerated towards us.

"Sharkey," I shouted to my friends. "He was the private detective *Rafe* hired to track me down! Rafe and Sharkey were in this together! But then Sharkey must have double-crossed my uncle!"

As the bulldozer came crashing through the archway, I pushed Boges and Winter out of the way.

Now the wall was bulging inwards—stones buckling in, sandy mortar pouring out. It would only be a matter of seconds before the entire western wall of Cragkill Keep fell, bringing the towers down.

I looked around for a way out. The exit at the end of the long gallery was too far away for us to make a run for it.

Somehow, I had to stop him. I had to stop the bulldozer.

I charged for it. I ran, ducking the stones that were falling from the archway. I was forced to leap to one side to avoid the bulldozer's scoop, raised and ready to bash me down.

I was faster than ever. I picked up a heavy stone and jumped on top of the housing of the caterpillar tracks. I smashed the window with the stone, wrenched open the door, then hurled myself on him, knocking him into the corner away from the controls.

"You murderer!" I yelled. "You killed my dad! How could you murder your own brother? Your own twin! You've tried to destroy my whole family! And *I* thought you'd come to *save* me from the oubliette! I thought you were the Ormond Angel coming to the aid of the heir! But you just wanted me alive a bit longer so I could lead you here to the treasure!"

My assault took him by surprise: It was the last thing he was expecting—he winced in pain, and I saw that his shirt was bloodstained—he *had* been shot. I threw myself on top of him, pinning him down. The rage that I'd felt earlier, simmering up through my body, exploded into homicidal fury. I wondered where the terrifying growling I could hear was coming from, until I realized it was me. I crashed Rafe as hard as I could against the side of the cab.

But now he'd recovered from the initial shock and was fighting back, enraged by the pain I'd inflicted on him. Blood trickled from his nose as he managed to free his arms, and he grasped me around the throat, trying to strangle me!

Instinctively, I lashed out, and his hold around my neck relaxed. It was just loose enough for me to twist sideways and with all my strength, pull myself away from him. I launched out of the cab, hit the ground hard and rolled over, getting to my feet again with intense speed. I ran back towards the Keep.

Rafe came after me, jumping out of the bulldozer, snarling. His lips were pulled back to show his teeth, deadly, like a werewolf in a horror movie. Behind us, the un-piloted bulldozer rose up against a pile of stones, crashing down again, closer and closer.

Boges and Winter raced towards us.

Rafe charged, falling on top of me, trying to hurl me back into the bulldozer's path, barely inches from the crushing tracks. I thumped the ground, winded. Getting my breath back, I fought as hard as I could, but I couldn't get any momentum behind my punches.

Again he had his hands around my throat. I rolled over the rough terrain, away from the tracks, twisting his hands, wrestling and gouging. Boges tried to help, tried to land a blow, but whenever he went to hit Rafe, somehow I was in the line of fire.

I could hear Winter yelling in the background, trying to wrench Rafe off me. Then I felt something thud hard on my legs. I looked down and saw what Winter had been trying to warn me about. A huge beam had fallen across my ankles, trapping me. I couldn't move.

Through my dazed vision, I saw Rafe jump up and pick up a huge rock. Winter tried to tackle him, but he shoved her away hard, sending her flying. I spotted Boges starting to charge him, but Rafe shoved him away too, with unbelievable strength.

My uncle stood above me, the crushing rock held high above him, the evil grin twisted into a snarl of demonic fury.

I tried to get up, but my legs were jammed under the wood. I was stuck.

Rafe was about to smash the rock down on my head.

Any second now, I'd be dead.

Goodbye Ormond Singularity. Goodbye everything. It would all be over in seconds.

A roaring sound caused Rafe to hesitate. He turned to look up as the massive second tower of Cragkill Keep finally caved and came crashing down in a thunderous avalanche. The huge stone carving we'd noticed earlier, broke free from the crumbling tower, falling and swooping down towards us. All I could do was flinch as it bore down . . . then landed . . . right on top of Rafe. The rock he was wielding flew out of his hands and skittered away as the oddly-shaped stone from the sky obliterated him and saved my life.

11:50 pm

Winter and Boges rushed over to free me, lifting the beam from my ankles. As they helped me up, Rafe lay motionless under the massive stone formation that had fallen on him, missing me by just inches. Beyond him, the bulldozer churned away, uselessly turning in a slow circle, jammed up against the pile of stones that once had been part of the walls of Cragkill Keep.

"Can you walk?" Boges asked me, helping me to my feet.

"Not sure yet," I said, trying. I looked down to see blood seeping through my jeans. I tried to walk, but almost fell.

"Dude, don't try to move. Just take it easy for a moment."

"You might have broken something," said Winter, kneeling beside me.

"What about Rafe?" I asked, alerted by a groaning noise and looking over at the outstretched figure under the massive stone.

He was alive. Just. Half of his face was pulped and almost unrecognizable. He made a sound—a hoarse, harsh noise in his throat.

"Cal," he was trying to say. "Help me."

"I want the truth," I replied, still trying to stand up.

My uncle groaned again.

"Film this, Boges," I said. "I want a full confession."

Boges whipped out his phone and selected the video function. "Start now, dude."

"Tell me everything," I ordered. "You killed my dad. You tried to kill me. Tell me everything. It'll go better for you in court."

"I don't think he's going to make it to court," Winter admitted, looking at his flattened body.

"Admit it *was* you who sabotaged the fishing boat that night out on Treachery Bay. It *was* you who sabotaged my life jacket."

"I did," he murmured. Boges leaned closer, making sure his words were captured on the recording.

"So that you could swim to shore safely with a story about how you'd tried to save me, but I'd tragically drowned," I continued.

Again, Rafe tried to nod and say yes.

"But you didn't take the storm into account. Then you set me up by attacking Gabbi and inflicting injuries on yourself. Making it look like I'd shot you. Admit it!"

"Yes," came the weak response. "Sharkey helped me. Please. Call an ambulance."

"Sharkey helped set it up?" murmured Winter, still in disbelief.

"And long before any of that, you hired Toe Cutter," I accused him, sick at the thought. I recalled the blueprints I'd found in his house, with an "X" marking one of the bedrooms. "It was you who organized for me and Samuel to be kidnapped, wasn't it?"

I could hear the sound of sirens coming our way. Had someone else alerted the police?

"Is that true?" I shouted at him.

"Yes," came the hoarse voice.

"What about my mum?" I asked him. "What really happened to start that fight the other day? Tell me!"

Rafe's eyes blinked. His chest barely moved up and down. His breath came in long, slow heaves. "She discovered that—"

"That what?"

"That I'd been replacing her herbal teas with—something else." His voice was so weak, I strained to listen. "Something that made her more *obedient* . . . made it easier for me to—"

"—to control her!" I finished for him. "You were poisoning her!" My face twisted in disgust. This man had been drugging my mum with one of his botanical toxins! No wonder she'd turned against me. "Is that all? There was something else she discovered, wasn't there?"

Rafe could hardly speak now. But I was

merciless. "Tell me!"

"She found them. Where I'd hidden them." He was struggling to breathe—his voice was nothing but strangled whispers. "The Ormond Jewel and the Riddle. Rathbone and I stole them from you. Please, Cal . . . get help."

"How could you do that to us? To your own family?"

"I just . . . wanted . . . out of the shadow . . ." he said.

"You let me think my mum hated me! That she believed I was a monster!"

"Your mother *loves* you . . . you fool."

And with that his head fell to the side, lifeless.

11:59 pm

I stared hard at the oddly-shaped statue that we'd finally managed to roll off Rafe.

Winter was staring at it too. "It has wings," she said. "Look."

She was right. It was the crumbling figure of a huge stone angel, worn by four hundred years of rain and wind.

"The Ormond Angel," I whispered, looking up at Winter.

"Came to the aid of the heir," she whispered, pulling me away from my uncle's body.

"Incredible, dude," Boges said, staring at the

fallen angel. "The stories were true. The Ormond Angel saved you."

In the distance, a village clock started chiming the hour. The chimes came slowly, the sweet sound of the bells echoing through the night.

One, two, three . . .

I had rightfully claimed the Ormond Singularity, just in time, and we had proof that Rafe had been behind the crimes I'd been accused of. I could go back to my country, and there'd be no more running, no more hiding, no more watching my back.

Even going back to school seemed like a great idea.

Four, five, six . . .

I thought of what I could do with the treasure I'd inherited. I could buy back our house in Richmond, and Mum would never have to worry about money ever again. I could pay back Boges for everything he'd done for me. I could give Repro some jewels to add to his collection and maybe even help reunite him with *his* mother.

Seven, eight, nine . . .

I slipped my arm around Winter's waist as the three of us turned back towards the floodlit ruins. Winter looked up at me with sparkling eyes. I really wanted to kiss her, but before I could, she hooked an arm around my neck, moved in close and on tiptoes, kissed *me*.

I'd make sure she would never have to think about Sligo ever again. She could go back to her family's house in Dolphin Point and start over. I held up her left wrist and softly kissed her bird tattoo. We could both start over. We were both finally free.

Ten, eleven . . .

Boges grinned and draped his arms over our shoulders. We all smiled at each other. Battered, filthy, exhausted and proud. I had two of the best friends a guy could ever wish for.

My team. My friends.

The last chime—twelve—echoed across the marsh, and then all was still and quiet. Midnight on the 31st of December. We'd done it. After 365 days, we'd finally done it.

I pictured Ryan, my lost twin. Now we had the rest of our lives to look forward to, together.

I pictured Mum, back to her old, happy self, free from Rafe and his poisons. She was in front of our house, welcoming me back, Gabbi beaming widely at her side. We'd be a family again.

Lastly, I pictured my dad. He was nodding at me.

"It's freezing," I said. "Let's go home."

Epilogue

31 JANUARY

Boges, Winter and I are home. It's January again, but a very different January from the last one.

I've been reunited with Gab and my mum—who's almost her old self again. We plan on buying back our Richmond house, and we can't wait to settle in and start getting to know Ryan Spencer. We're all looking forward to telling him stories about Dad and our amazing family history, and showing him the drawings that led me to the Ormond Singularity.

My new lawyer, Belinda Quick, is working on having all the charges against me dismissed.

I've taken care of Boges so that he, his mum and his gran, have everything they'll ever need. Boges is keen to get back to his studies—specializing in biometric systems and micro listening devices. He's also keen to ask out

Madeleine Baker, from school . . . but might need some tips from Winter.

Winter's staying with us. She's delivered evidence to the police, proving that Sligo caused the accident that killed her parents. Everything that belonged to her family will soon be returned to her. She's relieved, but convinced someone made it out of the Inisrue Marsh bog alive . . .

I returned to Repro's hideout with a jewel-filled pouch for him. He was speechless when he saw what was inside.

The Ormond Riddle and the Ormond Jewel are in a secure, secret location.

These days, I'm still being chased, but by people who want to know more about my life and the incredible DMO.

This is my story.